SIDECAR
STORIES

ANN MCMAN

D1516620

Bywater
BOOKS

Ann Arbor

Bywater Books

Bywater Books First Edition: July 2016

Sidecar was originally published by Beddazzled Ink, LLC
Fairfield, CA in 2012.

Printed in the United States of America
on acid-free paper.

Cover design by TreeHouse Studio

Bywater Books
PO Box 3671
Ann Arbor, MI 48106-3671

www.bywaterbooks.com

ISBN: 978-1-61294-087-8 Print
ISBN: 978-1-61294-088-5 Ebook

For SlumDog, who taught me to recognize
where a story really begins.

FOREWORD

"A hallucinogenic potato perfume, cassis, ripe berries, and acrid chocolate overtones are coalesced in this tough and chewy Muscadine from Beaver Glacier Estates—not," David said, as he poured the remaining wine down the drain with a flourish.

Maddie wiped her tongue with a wet paper towel. "What possessed you to set up a tasting with a wine rep from Southern Indiana?"

David sighed dramatically. "He said his wines were award winning."

Maddie raised an eyebrow. "Did you bother to ask if the awards were presented at a 4-H competition?"

Thus begins this feisty book of shorts by author, Ann McMan.

Well, not really.

But it could, and few loyal readers would be surprised. Come to think of it, no one who knows Ann McMan would be surprised. You see, contrary to chat room rumors, and speculation by puritanical reviewers on amazon.com, Ann isn't a foul-mouthed boozy lush—and she wasn't raised in the back room of the Hell's Angels MC Pennsylvania clubhouse.

The simple fact is that Ann McMan is very much like the women she writes about—razor sharp, intelligent, multi-faceted, funny, antagonistic towards spurious vegetables, and a little OCD. She has a soft spot for sweet dogs, adores opera, appreciates a well-made Cosmo, cooks up a mean batch of chicken and biscuits, and has a particular affinity for the F-Bomb. Sometimes she "gets that way she gets," and other times she doesn't. On very rare occasions, she channels Mrs. Trefoile in *Die! Die! My Darling!*

In all seriousness though, Ann McMan is a talented author with a special gift for timing and dialogue. She is a keen observer of the world around her, and excels at the sport of paying attention in the midst of chaos. The men and women who populate the landscapes of her books and stories are not only well rounded and complex, but familiar and psychologically believable—a rare and desirable combination in modern literature.

Oddly, not long after turning the manuscript for *Sidecar* over to her editor, Ann asked me to read through each of the stories, and to pay particular attention to her protagonists. "Do I keep writing the same characters over and over?" she asked. My first reaction was "Um…" Quickly followed by a "Well, maybe." Then I dodged the lime wedge she threw at me, and offered up a solid and convincing, "No, definitely not," before threatening to slip okra into her refrigerator if she didn't quit throwing fruit at me.

But I digress.

The real answer, the truthful answer is "Most assuredly not." While it's true that Ann's characters are universally smart, quick-witted, and clever, they each have distinct personalities, diverse perspectives, and skillfully hidden demons. Their voices reflect individual journeys and their divergent countenances color vividly across a wide spectrum. Try as I might, I have a hard time imagining *Jericho*'s Syd and Maddie eating a slice of lemon chess pie with Evan and Julia from Dust. Likewise, as I consider the cast of leading ladies within the pages of *Sidecar*, I think not of the similarities, but the differences between each of the women.

Of course, there's only one way to find out—you need climb in, get comfortable, and go for a quick ride with each of them. *Sidecar* gets things rolling with Syd and Maddie in "V1: A Valentine's Day Odyssey." Before you know it, you'll join the best and brightest authors in contemporary lesbian fiction at the year's biggest literary convention in the hilarious, gasp-provoking, all-new novella, "Bottle Rocket." From there, you'll travel coast-to-coast in "Falling from Grace," and finally you'll come to the end-of-the-line in the sweet and smart "Nevermore!."

Few things in life are certain, but I have absolutely no doubt that Ann McMan's *Sidecar* is the perfect vehicle for your journey—equal parts sweet, tart, and smooth.

Bottoms up!

Salem West
Publisher, Bywater Books

TABLE OF CONTENTS

V1:
A VALENTINE'S DAY ODYSSEY

"Okay. So tell me again how this is supposed to work."

"Syd, we've been over this about a thousand times." Maddie was growing exasperated, but was trying hard not to show it.

"I know—but I just need to be really sure."

"Sweetie, I've done everything but show you a PowerPoint presentation." Maddie hesitated. "You really don't have to do this at all if you're still this uncomfortable with the idea."

"No!" Syd was determined. "I said I'd do this, and I will. I'm just—"

"A chickenshit?" Maddie volunteered.

Syd glared at her. "Not helping."

"Sorry."

"I really don't think you are."

Maddie sighed. This was going from bad to worse in record time. She took hold of Syd's free hand. "No . . . I'm sorry. Honest."

Syd eyed her with suspicion.

"I mean it. If you want to go over everything again, we will. We can stop right now. There's no rush. We can do this any time. It doesn't have to be today."

Syd looked out the tiny window. Then she sighed and looked back at Maddie.

"It's just that it's such a big step for me."

"I know that, sweetheart."

"I mean . . . I've never done this before, and it's scary. What if I mess up? What if I can't make it work? What if I change my mind in the middle of it? What if—"

"Honey," Maddie said. "Relax. I promise . . . you won't mess up. I'll be right here beside you the whole time. Trust me. We've done everything right, and you're ready for this. You'll be through it in a flash, and then it'll be over, and our biggest problem will be how to keep you calmed down until you can do it again."

"But what if I can't pull it out?"

"Syd . . ."

"No. I mean it."

Maddie sighed and sat back against her seat. "Then I swear on the blonde heads of our unborn children that we'll take deep breaths, regroup, and try again."

"Are you sure?"

"Positive."

Syd sighed.

Maddie leaned toward her. "C'mon, baby. Let's go for it."

Syd nodded. She closed her eyes and started to extend her hand, but Maddie caught hold of it before it reached its destination.

"Honey," she said, giving Syd's hand a gentle squeeze. "This generally works better if you keep your eyes open."

"Oh." Syd looked embarrassed. "Sorry."

Maddie laughed and kissed her hand before relinquishing it.

Syd reached out again and took hold of the throttle levers. Taking a deep breath, she released her foothold on the brake pedals, and the twin engine Cessna started rolling down the runway.

That night at dinner, Henry was beside himself with excitement. He hammered Syd with a nonstop barrage of questions—most of them related to when he could learn to fly the airplane, too.

"Let's not get ahead of ourselves, shortstop." Maddie used her napkin to wipe some gravy off his chin. "And let's try to keep the peas on the fork, okay?"

Henry looked down and regarded the sea of tiny green balls that trailed across the napkin on his lap. "I don't really like peas very much."

Maddie leaned toward him until their foreheads touched. "Tough noogies."

Henry sighed and looked at Syd.

Syd shrugged. "Don't look at me, sport. I don't really like them either. But you don't see me dropping them on the floor."

"Pete likes them," he volunteered.

At the mention of his name, the big yellow dog lifted his head and cast a hopeful glance up at Henry. It hadn't taken him long to stake his claim to the section of kitchen floor that supported Henry's chair.

"Pete's on a diet," Maddie cut in. "And that's beside the point. We don't deal with food we don't like by giving it to Pete."

Henry looked confused. "But you did last night with your 'sparagus, when Syd had to go answer the phone."

Maddie closed her eyes and took a deep breath. When she dared to open them, Syd was staring back at her with pursed lips and was slowly tapping the edge of her fork against the rim of her plate.

"Um," Maddie said. "Asparagus is good for Pete. It has lots of iron and makes his coat shiny."

Henry looked unconvinced. "You said it would make him fart."

"Henry." Syd's jaw dropped, and she touched him on the shoulder. "That's impolite. We don't say things like that."

Henry looked really confused now. He stared down at his plate. "That's what she said," he muttered.

Syd glowered at Maddie, who sat across the table from her and felt like she'd rather be locked up in a supply closet with an insurance salesman.

The silence in the kitchen was deafening.

Then Maddie sighed and picked up her spoon.

"Here, buddy." She reached over to Henry's plate, scooped up a mound of peas, and dumped them onto the floor. "Lemme help you out."

Long after Henry had safely been tucked in, Maddie and Syd sat together on their big bed, propped up against a pile of mismatched pillows.

Maddie was reading an article about the efficacy of the Herpes Zoster Vaccine, and Syd was grading papers. She had been teaching for six months now, and was starting to settle into a comfortable routine. The Jericho Public Library had reopened, but only for three days a week, and Syd was able to assist the board with hiring a part-time branch manager. She continued to help out whenever she could and volunteered her time at least two Saturdays a month.

And Maddie still worked one weekend a month in the ER at the Wytheville Community Hospital.

Weekends were harder to orchestrate now, with Henry in the equation. He was like a floating decimal point in their lives. He belonged, but, while his father continued to serve out his tour of duty in Afghanistan, his position remained unfixed. And his presence changed everything.

Quiet evenings like this one were a rarity, and they were basking in the luxury of having a Saturday night at home together with no other commitments.

With a yawn, Syd capped her pen and shifted her stack of papers over to a bedside table.

Maddie glanced at her over the rim of her reading glasses. "You finished?"

Syd nodded. "For tonight. I'll finish these up tomorrow."

Maddie began to close her journal. "I can put this away, too."

"No, that's okay." Syd picked up her student pilot's flight manual. "I wanted to look through this a bit."

Maddie gave her a smug look. "You seem a tad more confident than you did earlier today."

"Smartass."

"Not at all. I just know you."

"You think so?"

"I know so." Maddie reopened her journal.

Syd sat chewing the inside of her cheek for a moment. Then she lowered her gaze to the flight manual and thumbed through its pages.

After a minute or two, Maddie noticed that Syd seemed to be turning more pages than she was reading—loudly.

She lowered her journal again. "You sure you don't want me to put this away?"

Syd faced her with raised eyebrows. "Are you talking to me?"

Maddie hooked an index finger over the bridge of her glasses and pulled them down her nose. "Is Robert De Niro hiding someplace in this bed? Of course I'm talking to you."

"Oh. Sorry. I didn't think you needed to ask me what I wanted."

Maddie sighed. "Could we hit the reboot button, please?"

12

"Why? You feel the need to take something back?"

"That depends."

"On?"

"On whether or not it'll get you to stop acting like Travis Bickle."

Syd smiled at that. "Have you ever even seen a movie that was made in this century?"

Maddie shrugged. "You got the reference."

Syd held up the aircraft manual. "Yes, but I don't get this one."

"Which one?"

Syd turned the book around so Maddie could see a diagram that illustrated the four-stroke process of an engine's piston and cylinder cycle.

"Internal combustion? That's just basic physics."

"Well, maybe it is to you, brainiac. But I don't get the whole squish, bang, pop, thing."

Maddie looked confused. "You mean, suck, squeeze, bang, and blow?"

"Exactly. There's nothing . . . intuitive about it."

Maddie closed her journal. "Sure there is."

Syd sighed. "Maybe it's just my learning style. I've always been better at hands-on instruction."

"Honey, there's really no way to get hands-on instruction in the operation of an internal combustion engine."

Syd ran a fingertip down the inside of Maddie's v-neck t-shirt. "Sure there is. You just have to be creative."

Maddie looked down at her hand. "Are we still talking about airplane engines?"

Syd moved closer. "Do you really care?" She pulled Maddie's glasses off and tossed them to the bedside table.

"Um . . . well . . ."

Syd kissed Maddie's neck.

Maddie felt her heart rate shift from idle into full-throttle mode. "I guess not."

"So, what were those stages again?" Syd breath was hot against Maddie's ear. She bit down on her lobe. "Suck?"

Maddie moaned and wrapped an arm around Syd. "Squeeze."

Their lips met.

"Bang?" Syd muttered against Maddie's mouth, as she pushed her back against the pillows and crawled on top of her.

13

Oh, Jesus. Zero to V1 in ten seconds. Maddie took hold of Syd's head, which was traveling down her torso at an accelerated rate of speed.

"Blow, baby," she gasped, while she could still make intelligible sounds. "Blow."

"You have got to be kidding me?" David was incredulous.

Maddie looked back at him with her characteristic, deadpan expression. "Do I look like I'm kidding?"

David considered that for a moment as he looked her up and down. "You can't show up here dressed like that and expect me to give you a serious answer."

Maddie looked down at her clothes. She had just finished an eight-hour shift in the Wytheville ER, and had stopped by the inn on her way home. Her blue scrubs were covered with iodine stains—the aftermath of going ten rounds with an anxious four-year-old who had vehemently—and vocally—resisted being the recipient of the nine stitches Maddie was obliged to apply to the gaping head wound the girl had sustained after riding her tricycle down the back steps of her parent's deck.

She looked around the completely empty dining room. Pretty typical for early February—which was why they closed the inn for the mid-winter months. She brought her eyes back to David.

"I apologize for committing the egregious error of not arriving in cocktail attire to sit here and watch paint dry."

"Well, I guess that's something." He plucked a piece of lint off his trouser cuff and re-crossed his legs. "Besides, I'm not watching paint dry, thank you very much. I'm just killing time until Chopped comes on."

Maddie looked back at him with a blank expression.

David sighed. "If you weren't such an unrepentant Philistine, you'd know these things."

"Whatever. May we return to my original query, please?"

"We may ... but I still think you've lost it. She'll never buy it. And, besides, there's no way you can pull this off."

"Thanks for the vote of confidence, Davey."

He waved a hand toward her. "I'm just trying to help you out, Cinderella."

"By undermining my confidence?"

"No. By helping you face reality."

Maddie sat back against her chair. "That's simply ridiculous. I certainly have the skill set to pull this off."

David leaned forward. "Oh really? I have two words for you, Sparky."

Maddie lifted her chin.

"Easy Bake. Not."

"That's three words."

He rolled his eyes. "You know what I'm talking about. You damn near burned down the farm with that thing, and, may I add, that oven was only powered by a fucking light bulb. It boggles the mind to think about what kind of damage you could do on Michael's precious, eight-burner, turbo-powered Bertazzoni."

Maddie sighed. "Look. It's Syd' birthday, and I want to cook dinner for her."

David shook his head. "I don't get it. I thought you two were doing great."

"We are doing great."

"Then explain to me why you want to kill her?"

Maddie exhaled. "I may not have to kill her if I can satisfy my bloodlust by eviscerating your ass. Now, will you help me out or not?"

"Why are you even asking me for help? It's Michael you need, not me."

"I'll get around to him, but I need you on board, first."

"Yeah . . . on board. Perfect image. Just like the Titanic's maiden voyage."

"David . . ."

He shook his head. "I know I'll live to regret this, but, okay. I'll help you."

Maddie sat back and smiled.

David took a sip from his glass of wine. "Now, pray tell, what part will I be playing in this little Greek tragedy?"

"Ah," Maddie said, as she tented her fingertips. "You'll be cast true to type."

David eyed her with suspicion. "As?"

Maddie shrugged. "My alibi, of course."

"Your alibi?"

"Yeah."

David exhaled in frustration.

Maddie pressed her advantage. "Oh come on. It's not like you don't have experience at this."

"Sure . . . but convincing your father those copies of Playboy he found stashed under the sofa cushions belonged to me was a cakewalk, compared to this."

"Now, why do you say that?"

"Hello? Seen the woman you've been keeping company with, Cinderella? Isn't she now like some kind of brown belt in Tae Kwon Do, or something?"

"Green belt. But what's your point?"

"My point is that I value my gonads. And I know Syd. If she suspects that you're up to something clandestine—and that I'm protecting you—she'll body slam me first and ask questions later."

Maddie was growing impatient with this. "In the first place, if Syd ever body slams you, you'll be too . . . titillated to care about anything else. In the second place, I promise not to let it go that far. I only need an alibi for a couple of nights. Her birthday is in two weeks, as it is."

"I know when her birthday is. I remember last year, Miss 'Oh, by the way, I'm gay.' I'm still pissed at you about that little Valentine's Day revelation."

Maddie sighed. "I've apologized to you for that. A lot of times, if memory serves. Can I help it if it came out before you were able to join us?"

"Yeah. All kinds of things came out that night."

Maddie made no response, but sat drumming her fingertips on the tabletop. They stared at each other. All they lacked were ambient cricket noises.

David blinked first. "Okay. All right. I'll do it."

Maddie gave him one of her most brilliant smiles. Then she sat back and told him the details of her plan.

Michael was a harder sell.

It was his kitchen, after all, and Michael was very . . . specific about his kitchen. And especially about his stove.

"I don't know about this," he said, as he regarded Maddie with crossed arms. "What were you thinking about making?"

16

"I have a few thoughts," she replied.

"Like?" he prompted.

Maddie sighed. "What difference does it make?"

"You're joking, right? It makes a huge difference. I mean, honestly, Maddie. Sauces alone can take months, even years to perfect."

Maddie rolled her eyes toward the ceiling.

"Oh, don't think I didn't see that, Dr. Strangelove. Being able to cut up a cadaver with your ham fists and your crude medical implements doesn't automatically qualify you to prepare a perfectly proportioned platter of crudités."

"Fine. I'll buy precut vegetables."

Michael stared at Maddie like she had just suggested they roast a goat on his range—without a drip pan.

"Okay, okay," she offered, in her most conciliatory voice. "We'll do it your way. What do you want to know?"

"For starters, what kind of cuisine, and how many courses?"

Maddie hauled up a stool and sat down. Clearly, this was going to be a long conversation.

"I was thinking . . . French."

Michael gasped.

"And, maybe, four courses?"

Michael paled. "Four?"

Maddie nodded.

"Only four? Why not six? Why not eight? Why not just drive a stake through my heart and get this nightmare over with now?"

Maddie sighed. "You know . . . I'm not an imbecile." She fluttered her hands in front of him. "Look. I actually have opposable thumbs. And I did manage to graduate at the top of my med school class."

Michael still looked unconvinced.

Maddie decided it was time to haul out the big guns.

"It's for Syd, Michael. Help me do this for her?"

He folded like a cheap suit. Then he sighed and sat down on a stool, facing Maddie. "All right, but with one condition."

"What's that?"

"I need time to have the deductible lowered on our fire insurance."

"Very funny."

"Come on," Michael gestured at the file folder in Maddie's hand, "Show me what you got."

17

Maddie finally pulled into her barn at home well after eight that night and parked her Jeep next to Syd's Volvo. She regretted that she'd missed dinner with Henry—although she'd called Syd from the hospital to tell her she'd be late. She just hadn't volunteered the reason why, choosing to let Syd draw her own conclusions.

This was going to be the hard part—inventing reasons for her absences from home while she worked on honing her culinary skills with Michael.

Shit. Maybe David was right, and I should just let them cater the whole damn meal?

No. She wanted to do this for Syd. After all, Syd was willingly leaving her own comfort zone to learn how to fly. Learning how to cook one decent meal seemed like the least she could do to pay her back. It would be a selfless and loving quid pro quo.

At least, she hoped so.

She glanced at the workbench in her barn. Edna Freemantle's toaster oven sat there—in about five pieces. Edna dropped it while trying to empty its crumb tray, and she desperately wanted Maddie to fix it, even though Maddie told her it would be cheaper to just go to Walmart and buy a new one. But Edna refused, and now Maddie was waiting on replacement parts to arrive from . . . someplace.

Damn David for reminding her about that regrettable incident with her Easy Bake oven. How was she supposed to know that it wouldn't work with pizza rolls? Those damn things went up like mini Roman candles. Her parents punished her for weeks. She remembered that Celine was furious with her, but she thought her father had a hard time concealing his grudging pleasure that she had expressed a desire to try and cook anything. She shook her head and walked on toward the house.

Pete met her at the kitchen door. She let him outside before taking off her jacket and announcing, "I'm home!"

"We're up here." Syd's voice carried down the back stairs.

Maddie took the steps two at a time. They were down the hall, in Henry's room—the big room at the front of the house that had been Maddie's when she was a girl. Henry was already under the covers. He was wearing his sock monkey pajamas—a Christmas gift from Celine—and Syd was reading to him.

Maddie bent over and kissed Henry on the head, then turned and kissed Syd. "Hello my little family. I missed you both tonight."

Syd smiled at her. "We missed you, too. Did you get some dinner?"

"Yes. I grabbed something on the way home." She looked at Henry. "How was your day, sport?"

"I got to ride in a fire truck, Maddie. And I got to make the siren go."

"You did? How did that happen, pal?"

"They came to my school. They told us not to start fires."

Maddie nodded. "That's very good advice, Henry. I hope you never will."

She was glad David wasn't present to hear this conversation.

Syd was staring at the stains on Maddie's scrubs. "Do I want to know what that is on your clothes?"

"It's iodine." Maddie sighed. "I went ten rounds with a four-year-old who needed stitches. Believe me when I tell you that she fared much better than I did."

Syd laughed. "Why don't you go change, then, and I'll put those in to wash?"

"What's eye-dine, Maddie?" Henry asked, with wide eyes.

Maddie sat down on the edge of his bed. "It's a yucky, brownish liquid that we use to clean cuts and boo-boos before we can sew them up."

"I don't want any of that," he said.

"Then be very careful, and maybe you'll never have to have any."

"Okay."

"Why don't I stay here while Syd finishes reading your story?" Maddie looked at her Syd. "Syd never reads to me anymore."

Syd raised an eyebrow. "I don't really have to read to you anymore. You generally find other ways to unwind before bedtime."

Maddie cleared her throat. "On the other hand, why don't I go and change out of these dirty clothes?" She stood up and kissed Henry again. "I'll come back to listen to the rest of your story, Henry, and to say goodnight."

"Okay, Maddie." He shifted his small frame around in the big bed and pulled the blankets up closer to his chin.

Maddie ran a hand down Syd's back as she walked toward the door. "And I'll come up with something special for you, blondie," she whispered.

19

Syd leaned into her hand. "Oh, I just bet you will, stretch."

As she was walking back down the wide center hallway toward the master suite, she smiled as she heard the soft tones of Syd's voice as she read to Henry.

"On the fifteenth of May, in the Jungle of Nool . . ."

Maddie fared pretty well coming up with convincing explanations for her cascade of evening commitments—at least for the first three sessions with Michael. By the fourth night, Syd was beginning to chafe at her continued absences and was struggling to contain her growing concern about what might really be behind them. It didn't help that once or twice, she'd walked in on Maddie while she was engrossed in phone conversations with someone, and Maddie's reflexive and abrupt efforts to terminate the calls only ratcheted up Syd's anxiety about what might be driving Maddie to be so illusive and secretive about her nocturnal activities.

But Syd was a mature woman, and she reminded herself that she loved and trusted Maddie, and had no reason to suspect that Maddie was up to anything . . . untoward.

She didn't, did she?

Of course not. She understood that the biggest part of what drove her to worry about Maddie's unusual behavior was her own ill-fated tenure as the spouse of a philandering husband.

But Maddie wasn't Jeff—not by any stretch of the imagination. And she knew that her reactions and fears were reflexive, and not rational.

Still, her conscience argued, what would the harm be to check it out?

Her first course of action simply would be to ask Maddie about it—circumspectly, of course. She didn't want to appear paranoid or over-anxious. Needy would also be bad. She wanted to avoid that appearance as well.

Even though "needy" pretty much summarized how she was starting to feel.

She got her chance to broach the subject when they met for an impromptu lunch on Thursday. Maddie had a long break between appointments that day and called Syd at the high school to see if she could sneak away before her afternoon orchestra practice to grab a fast bite at Freemantle's market. Syd agreed at once, and the two of them sat close together at a small table behind a towering display of motor oils and fuel injector cleaners.

They dined on the inevitable hot dogs and Diet Coke.

Syd finished hers and licked a stray drizzle of chili from her fingertips. "I'll live to regret this."

Maddie withdrew a foil-wrapped pill from her pocket. Smiling, she slid it across the tabletop. "Here you go. I raided the supply closet."

Syd picked it up and examined it. "And this would be?"

"Twenty milligrams of Famotidine."

"Just what the doctor ordered?"

"Just what this doctor ordered—at least, for you."

"Why, thank you. I wish my other needs were as easily met."

Maddie raised an eyebrow. "Really? That sounds ominous."

"I wouldn't say ominous, exactly."

"Well, whatever you would say, I'd be happy to hear about it."

"Do you mean that?"

Maddie's blue eyes looked genuinely concerned now. "Of course I mean that." She extended a hand and rested it on Syd's forearm. "What's up, honey?"

Maddie's worried expression made Syd feel awkward . . . and ashamed of her suspicions. She laid a hand on top of Maddie's and gave it a squeeze.

"It's nothing. I'm just being silly."

"It's not nothing if you're worried about something. What is it? Come on, sweetie. It's me." She smiled at her. "Sit back and tell me where it hurts."

Syd sighed. "I'm embarrassed to tell you."

"Syd—"

"No. Let me finish." Syd twisted her Diet Coke can around while she tried to find the right words to ask Maddie about what was really on her mind.

Maddie slid her chair closer and took hold of Syd's hand. "Okay. You're really starting to scare the shit out of me."

Syd gazed at her. God, the woman was drop-dead gorgeous. She still took her breath away. There were a thousand things she wanted to say.

"I love you," she said instead, opting for the only one that really mattered.

Maddie eyes softened. "I love you, too."

"I know you do." And she did know it—in her viscera, where real truth resided. She shook her head. "It's nothing. I think I'm just hormonal as hell. And all these make-up snow days are driving the kids nuts, and they're all getting on my last nerve. I'm just . . . tense."

"Tense?" Maddie looked unconvinced.

"Yeah. Tense. Honest."

"That's it? The stuff at school?"

Syd nodded.

"Nothing at home? Nothing with Henry? Nothing with us?"

Syd smiled and squeezed her hand. "Never."

Maddie exhaled and sat back in her chair. "Well, thank god." She lowered her voice and said in conspiratorial tones, "Lucky for you, I did a standard rotation in stress relief. I think I can help you out with your problem."

"My problem?" Syd was beginning to think that approaching Maddie about her tension might prove to be one of her better ideas. "Do tell, Doctor. I'm all ears."

Maddie gave her a look that was anything but chaste. "Once again, I'm happy to point out that you are anything but."

"I'm suddenly feeling very dirty."

"Again, lucky for you. I have a cure for that, too."

Syd was preparing to ask Maddie when and how she might prove the veracity of her claims when Maddie's cell phone rang.

She answered it.

After a short conversation, Maddie pushed back her chair and stood up. "I'm going to have to run off, honey. That was Peggy. Zeke Dawkins sliced his hand open with a box cutter, and he's at the clinic now."

Syd smiled at her. "It's okay, Dr. Kildare. I know where you live."

Maddie squeezed her shoulder. "You certainly do. And I'll see you there later on."

"Count on it."

Syd watched her go, wondering what she had ever been worried about.

Maddie wasn't at all lacking in sensibility where Syd was concerned, and after their lunch conversation, she almost gave up on her double-whammy, Birthday cum Valentine's Day Culinary Extravaganza. She said as much to Michael the next day when they met over coffee at Dunkin' Donuts to confer about the details of their next practice session, but Michael encouraged her boldly to soldier on.

"You can't stop now," he said. "We're at a crucial stage. Tonight, we clarify butter. And you know how important that is. The success or failure of this entire enterprise hangs in the balance. If you walk away now . . . well. I can't even find the words to describe the breadth of disappointed hopes you'll leave in your wake."

Maddie looked at him in wonder. "You sound like we're planning the invasion of Normandy. It's only a birthday dinner, Michael."

He stared at her with an open mouth.

"Hello?" Maddie prompted, snapping her fingers in front of him. His face looked like it was etched in stone.

"Never was so much owed by so many to so few." His voice was a whisper.

"Oh, please. You're not seriously playing the Churchill card? Can we dial this back a bit?"

He crossed his arms. "I don't see how. Not when you seem determined to cast aspersion on my entire craft."

"Oh, come on. Syd thinks I'm cheating on her, for god's sake. I just can't keep this deception up." She sighed and shook her head. "I should've listened to David."

Michael reached across the table and slapped her. "Snap out of it." His voice rang out across the restaurant.

Stunned, Maddie raised a hand to her cheek and looked at him like he had suddenly sprouted horns. Patrons at other tables turned around in their seats to stare at the two of them.

"What the hell was that for?" she hissed.

"For saying you should have listened to David."

"Oh." Maddie rubbed her cheek as she considered that. "Thanks. You're right."

Michael nodded and picked up his cup of coffee.

Maddie turned to the other diners. "Finish your donuts, folks. There's nothing else to see here."

Slowly, the other patrons returned their attention to their lattes and Bavarian Kreme Sticks.

Maddie turned back to Michael. "By the way, big guy. Nice job channeling Cher."

He smiled at her.

"I guess attending all forty-two of those farewell tours finally paid off."

"I'll say." He leaned forward. "Now, about tonight . . ."

When Maddie called Syd late on Friday afternoon to say she'd be out again, Syd gave up trying to be understanding and not jump to conclusions. She'd had it, and all bets were off.

Maddie said she'd been called in to help Tom Greene out in the ER that night—that the plague of upper respiratory crud that had been blazing a trail across the county had finally hit the hospital staff, and half of Tom's employees had called in sick. She said she'd try not to be too late and apologized profusely for missing yet another evening at home with Syd and Henry.

Syd opened her mouth to protest when Maddie cut her off.

"I gotta run, sweetie. This waiting room looks like Walmart on the Friday after Thanksgiving. I love you."

She hung up.

Syd stood there fuming, holding the phone against her ear. Before she could talk herself out of it, she hung up, then punched in the number for Freemantle's Market.

"Hello, Edna? It's Syd Murphy. Do you happen to know if Roma Jean is available tonight? I need a sitter for Henry . . ."

"I can't believe I let you talk me into this. I'm freezing my ass off."

Syd glared at him. "Will you quit complaining? There was no way I was going to sit out here in the dark by myself."

David pulled his fur-trimmed car coat tighter across his neck. "Can't we at least turn the damn heat on?"

"No."

"Why the hell not?"

"I told you. I don't wanna steam up the windows."

"Right. You're afraid that any damn polar bears that wander by in search of food might mistake our frozen corpses for ringed seals?"

"You know . . . you'd stay warmer if you'd shut up."

"How long are we gonna sit out here?"

"Until she comes out."

He sighed. "And then what?"

"We've been over this already."

"And?"

"And . . . we follow her."

David drummed his gloved fingers on the center console of Syd's Volvo. This was shaping up to be a bona fide nightmare. And he was caught right in the middle of it.

When Syd called him and said she was on her way over to pick him up, he grilled her about why. What she said made his hair stand on end. He shot a quick text message off to Maddie.

The eagle has landed. Goldks headed to big house to catch Mama Bear with fingers in porridge bowl.

In exactly ninety seconds, Maddie called him back.

"Would you mind translating that message into English, please?"

He sighed. "Syd is on her way to stake out the damn hospital. She wants to find out what you're really up to, and she's dragging my ass along with her."

"What?"

"You heard me. So you'd better come up with an alibi fast."

"David, that's your damn job!"

"Hey. You can't pin this one on me, Cinderella. I'm an innocent bystander. And one, I might add, who now deserves hazardous duty pay."

"Shit."

"Tell me about it. Look. You need to figure something out. Fast. She'll be here in about five minutes, and I have to change."

"Change?"

"Duh?" He sighed. "I can't go on a stakeout in February wearing poly-blend. I need flannel." He paused. "What kind of lesbian are you, anyway?"

"Oh, good god." She hung up.

That was two grueling hours ago, and David was certain that his caps were going to crack from how much his teeth were chattering.

He thought he'd try again to talk Syd down off her ledge of suspicion.

"Look," he began. "This is really a fool's errand. I know Maddie. Believeme. She's incapable of cheating."

Syd brought her eyes to bear on him like the laser beam sight of a shotgun. "Cheating? Who said anything about her cheating?"

Fuck. "Forget I said that. Bad, bad choice of words."

Her eyes narrowed. "What do you know?"

He threw up his hands. "Nothing. I know nothing."

"Right, Sergeant Schultz." She grabbed him by the lapels of his jacket. "Give it up. Now."

"Syd." He slapped at her hands. "Do you mind? Careful with the ermine." He brushed down the fur collar of his jacket. "I told you. I don't know anything."

"Then why are you so anxious to get me to give this up?"

"Because my lips are turning a hideous shade of puce. It's freezing out here."

She sighed and sat back against her seat. "All right. I'll start the car and turn on the heat . . . briefly. Just long enough to take the chill off. But in exchange, you fess up and tell me what the hell she's up to. And don't lie to me and say you don't know anything, or I might just slip up and tell your mother about some of the more eclectic interlibrary loan items I've had to procure for you from the state prison collection."

He could feel the blood drain from his face. "You wouldn't dare."

She leaned toward him. "Oh, I promise you, I would."

"That's blackmail. Isn't that against your creed?"

"Librarians don't have a creed."

"Oh, nice. Great time to tell me that."

She lifted her hand and placed it on the ignition. "So. Whattaya say? A little tit for tat?"

He rolled his eyes. "Not the most effective phrase to use with a gay man."

"You get my drift."

He sighed. "All right already. I'm so fucking cold I'd agree to do a pole dance in a pair of your father's hip waders to get you turn on the damn heat."

She shook her head and started the car. They sat there in blissful silence for a few minutes as the passenger compartment warmed up, and the windows fogged over.

David stretched his cramped legs out and sighed contentedly as warmth flooded over his body. Down the hill, across the parking lot from where they sat, the big glass door that led into the ER lobby opened. He stared as two figures emerged and headed straight toward them. Panic raced over his frame.

"Oh, Jesus H. Christ!"

"What now?" Syd looked at him.

"Tom Greene at ten o'clock. Headed straight for us."

"What?"

David frantically pointed out the windshield.

"Oh, shit."

"Yeah."

"What do we do?"

"Do? How the hell do I know? Think of something."

"Me?"

"Yes, you. This whole ridiculous stakeout was your insane idea." David was nearly hysterical. "Oh, shit, he sees us. I know he does. That old letch will never let us live this one down. How will we ever explain—"

Syd grabbed David and hauled him across the console so he was half lying on top of her. She pressed her lips to his in a passionate kiss.

Shocked and addled, David fought against her. His wild arm gestures only succeeded in knocking the car's gearshift lever into drive. Their wrestling match on the front seats continued while the car rolled out of its parking space, and quickly gained momentum as it rolled downhill and straight into the path of an inbound ambulance. The front airbags deployed and separated them with astonishing force.

Then Syd's car alarm went off.

Medical personnel flooded out of the ER and into the parking lot. Steam rolled out from beneath the crushed hood of Syd's car. People were running and shouting. Orderlies ran toward them with gurneys. The front end of Syd's car was now wedged beneath the bumper of a Wythe County EMT wagon.

Dazed, Syd and David broke their clinch and looked at each other.

"Fuck," they said in unison.

The parking lot was like a production number from a Busby Berkeley musical. People were crawling all over the place. In the five minutes since the accident, it seemed that police cars from nine departments had shown up and blocked them in.

"How many fucking donut shops are there in this damn county?" David complained.

Syd felt like time had stopped, and they had been sitting inside the car for at least a decade. She had a sick feeling that life, as she knew it, would never be the same.

A gentle tapping against the driver's side window finally got her attention. Slowly, inevitably, she turned toward the fateful sound to see Maddie standing outside the car and peering in at them with crossed arms and an unreadable expression.

Syd slowly rolled down her window. "Um. Hi."

Maddie cleared her throat, and just stood there saying nothing. In this case, Maddie saying nothing, managed to speak volumes. Syd was amazed at how much she looked like her mother right then.

Not a good sign at all.

"I suppose you're wondering what we're doing here?" Syd asked, meekly.

"No," Maddie finally said. "I think that part is pretty obvious. Why you're here, however, is likely to remain one of life's great unsolved mysteries."

Syd just stared back at her in abject silence.

Maddie sighed. "I think there are some gentlemen here who are eager to talk with you." She turned her head to indicate two Sheriff's deputies who stood near the hospital entrance, tapping their pens against open notepads and staring at the carnage.

Maddie then took a step back and opened Syd's car door. "Lucy, perhaps you and Ethel would care to join us inside, so we can discuss this little sitcom?"

Syd looked at her partner in crime, who was busy trying to brush white airbag dust off his fur collar. He raised his head and met her hopeless gaze.

"Don't look at me, Mrs. Ricardo. I'm just the sidekick. You're the one with the 'splaining to do."

It was after ten that night when Maddie paid Roma Jean and thanked her for spending the evening with Henry. To her credit, Roma Jean managed to thank Maddie, take the cash, and stumble out of the house without tripping over anything.

Progress, indeed.

Syd's Volvo had been towed to the Firestone garage in Jericho, and she had ridden home with Maddie in the Jeep. Silently.

They had dropped an equally silent David off at the inn on their way back to the farm. When Maddie smiled and wished him a good night's sleep, he shot her the bird and muttered, "Paybacks, Cinderella. Paybacks."

Syd watched him trot up the steps to the inn and leave a trail of white dust in his wake.

"What did he mean by that?"

Maddie looked at her. "Oh. So you're talking to me now?"

"No."

Maddie chuckled. "My mistake."

Syd didn't respond.

Now Syd was upstairs showering. Maddie could hear the water running as she walked to Henry's room to tuck him back in.

Henry had a tendency to kick his blankets off, and then wake up cold during the night. Maddie entered his room and smiled. Pete was sound asleep on the foot of his bed. Since Henry came to stay with them, Pete had more or less taken up residence in Henry's room. The two were inseparable.

Maddie adjusted his covers. Henry rolled over and opened his eyes. He gave her a sleepy smile.

"Hi, Maddie."

"Hi, Sport." She sat down on the edge of his bed. "Did you have fun tonight with Roma Jean?"

He nodded. "We ate pizza and watched American Idol."

Maddie smiled. "Did you do your homework?"

"Yes." He nodded. "I did it with Syd before Roma Jean came."

Maddie smiled. "Good." She ran a hand over his tousled hair. "I'm sorry I've been gone so much lately. I want you to know that I miss you and Syd when I'm not here."

"We miss you, too." He yawned. "Gramma C. called."

He meant Celine.

"She did?"

He nodded. "She said she would call back."

"Did she say anything else?"

"She said she was coming for Easter." He seemed excited at first, then he frowned. "She said she had a new piano book for me."

Maddie tried not to laugh. "You go back to sleep now, sport. We'll talk about it at breakfast, okay?"

"Okay, Maddie." He rolled over and pushed his head down into his pillow. "I love you."

"I love you, too, buddy." She kissed his head.

She scrubbed Pete's ears, then left his room to head for the master suite at the opposite end of the hall.

The water had stopped running, so Syd must have finished with her shower.

Maddie paused at the doorway to the room, deliberating about what to do.

"Are you going to stand there all night, or are you going to get in here and join me?"

Syd's voice came from around the corner. Apparently, she was still in the bathroom.

At least she was talking now. That had to be a good sign.

Maddie walked into the bedroom and rounded the corner into the bathroom. It was illuminated by candlelight, and Syd reclined in the big garden tub, wearing nothing but a sultry smile.

"Um," Maddie began. "Did I miss a few plot points?"

Syd lazily trailed her hand through the sudsy water. "I can't think of any points you've ever missed."

Maddie sat down on the edge of the tub. "Not that I'm complaining or anything, but I confess to being a little—"

"Confused?" Syd suggested.

"Yeah. That about covers it."

"Well, how about you shuck off your clothes and climb in here? I'm sure I can clear everything up for you in record time."

Maddie pinched herself. "Nope. I'm still awake." She looked at Syd in amazement. "An hour ago, you wanted to kill me."

Syd ran a hand along Maddie's arm. "No. An hour ago, I wanted to kill myself for being so stupid. And for giving in to a ridiculous, irrational, and paranoid delusion."

Maddie narrowed her eyes. "Is this horrifying characterization of your mental state supposed to make me feel better?"

"No." Syd sat up and took hold of Maddie's head and tugged her forward until their lips were nearly touching. "This is." She ran the tip of her tongue across Maddie's lips, then kissed her, and slowly untied the drawstring on the pants of Maddie's blue scrubs.

When they finally drew apart, Maddie's head was spinning, but things were definitely getting clearer. A lot clearer.

"I'm sorry for being such an idiot," Syd whispered.

Maddie was too busy pulling off the rest of her clothes and climbing into the tub to hear any more of her apology.

Maddie settled into the tub beside Syd, who slid over to straddle her lap. "Think you can ever forgive me?"

"Well, I—" Maddie wrapped one arm around her and latched onto the side the tub with her free hand, just so they could stay above water.

Syd's lips now were busy expressing the nonverbal portion of her apology, and Maddie was learning how easily breathing could become a foreign concept.

"I uh . . ."

Coherent thought appeared to have left the building, too.

"If I did forgive you, I guess that would make me—"

"All wet?" Syd asked, innocently—although what she was doing beneath the surface of the water was anything but innocent.

Oh my god.

Forming complete sentences was now a lost art. Another minute passed.

"Yes . . . yes," Maddie finally managed. "All wet."

Syd smiled against her mouth. "That makes two of us."

The hell with it.

Maddie let go of the tub, and they both slid deeper into the water.

February 14th. D-Day

It wasn't going well.

Not at all.

And Syd's birthday dinner was tonight.

Maddie was flying solo because, way back in December, Michael had picked up a catering gig for a wedding reception in Jefferson, and he couldn't get out of it. He promised her that he'd be back in plenty of time to oversee most of what they had on tap for the evening, but Maddie was charged with doing the initial prep work and getting a jump-start on the dessert course: a pumpkin custard tart with red-wine caramel sauce. Her job was to premix the dough mixture so it could

31

refrigerate—it apparently required two hours to do whatever-in-the-hell-it-was-that-dough-had-to-do in the refrigerator—and make the custard filling. All this, so they could be ready to assemble the actual tarts when Michael returned.

There was just one problem. She got held up at the clinic when Lizzy called to say she'd be late getting back from Blacksburg, where she'd celebrated an early Valentine's Day with Syd's brother, Tom. That meant Maddie had been unable to be at the inn by noon, as she'd planned. So she found herself in a time crunch, and didn't have the requisite two hours to wait for the dough to properly . . . do whatever.

Her clothes for the evening—and her overnight bag—were already there. All Syd knew was that they were meeting at the inn for a Valentine's Day/birthday dinner. She had no idea that Maddie was cooking, or that they would also be spending the night there, alone, in the very biggest and best guest suite. And this time, there'd be no red, Dr. Denton footie pajamas in the equation.

There'd be no pajamas at all, if she played her cards right.

Lizzy was keeping Henry overnight at her place. Syd didn't know that part yet, either.

Maddie told Syd that she had late appointments at the clinic, and that she'd have to meet her at the inn. She made a grand ceremony out of carrying a garment bag containing a change of clothes with her when she left home that morning, and she told Syd that she'd change at the clinic. Syd didn't seem to question this. And if she was harboring any nascent suspicions, she was still enough enmeshed in atonement mode from the whole demolition derby stunt at the hospital that she bravely kept them to herself.

Now Maddie was running about five hours behind schedule, and she needed to make some hard choices.

Well, she reasoned, when something doesn't fit, you make adjustments. Right? Cooking, after all, was a science. Just like medicine . . . or small appliance repair. It shouldn't be rocket science to puzzle this one out. Really. So she glanced at the clock and thought about how to make this work.

First, the dessert.

Why not just premix everything together and then toss the whole thing into the freezer? That would expedite the setting up process—cutting the time down by at least half. Maybe even two-thirds?

Michael would never know the difference, and she'd be right on track for them to finish the tarts, and start the Daube de Boeuf a la Saintongeaise, which Michael said needed to be prepared a day ahead of time and reheated, for best results, but they'd have to make do with half a day.

Whatever.

She also thought she could get a jump-start on the French Vinaigrette with Hard-Boiled Egg Dressing for the grilled, bacon-wrapped asparagus appetizer—a concession, and an apologetic offering for the recent, regrettable incident with Pete.

Like any good clinician, she assembled her tools and ingredients first.

She was a whiz at multitasking, and knew it, so she didn't worry too much about Michael's solemn admonition that she needed to concentrate on completing one task at a time. Hell, she could single-handedly juggle multiple gunshot wounds, gang fights, drug over-doses, and crazy indigents pissing in the water fountains in the Presby ER on any Saturday night. This should be like a walk in the spring rain.

She looked at her watch again. Damn. It was two-thirty. Syd would be there in less than four hours.

Okay. First things first. The dough.

Well . . . maybe the eggs. Those she could set to hard boil while she started the pastry mix.

Oh, and the meat. That needed to be at room temperature. She walked to the big walk-in cooler and grabbed the two pounds of beef shin she'd bought at the butcher shop in Roanoke. She also grabbed the fat slabs of bacon they'd need to wrap the asparagus. Correction: it was pancetta, not bacon. Michael was quick to correct her when she showed up with the wrong damn side meat and had to go back to the store. Again. Hell, she was practically a shareholder in that joint now.

So. Okay. The eggs.

She took a heavy, stainless steel and copper pan down from the pot rack that hung over the kitchen's big center island and put a couple of inches of water into it. She only needed one egg for the dressing, but decided to go ahead and hard boil six or seven. Why waste a whole pan of water for one damn egg? Besides, she liked hard-boiled eggs, and they could always use them for something else.

Once the eggs were nicely going, she carried her pastry and filling items to the area where the big, gunmetal gray mixer stood, proud and gleaming, like some kind of culinary obelisk. Michael practically

33

worshipped the damn thing. He even had a name for it—Gloria.

G-L-O-R-I-A. Yeah. That one.

She paused to look over the recipe.

Fuck.

The damn eggs were supposed to be at room temperature, too.

No problem. She'd wait just a few minutes, then grab a couple out of the hot water on the stove. That should work just fine, as long as she got them out before the water started to boil.

In the meantime, she could start chopping and combining the spices.

Okay . . . ginger . . . check. Almonds . . . check. Cloves . . . check. White pepper . . . check. Whole beans of has-to-be-grated nutmeg . . . check. Cardamom . . . shit. Cardamom. God damn it! She forgot the cardamom. She looked up at the ceiling and took a deep breath. Then she squared her shoulders.

Substitution.

That's what the best chefs did.

They always did it.

Okay. What would work instead of cardamom? It was a mainstay of Indian cuisine, right? So that meant it was spicy. It was one of the key ingredients in garam masala—a seasoning Maddie loved. So what was like that? She walked to Michael's spice cabinet and looked it over.

Curry.

That should work. That was in garam masala, too. Okay, curry powder it is.

She walked back to the mixer.

Shit . . . the eggs.

Well. The water had only just started to roll, so they were probably still okay.

She grabbed a sieve-style spoon and scooped three of them out and carried them to the table next to "Gloria's" mixer altar.

Okay. Let's see. She looked over the instructions.

> Pulse almonds, flour, baking powder, salt, and spices in a food processor until nuts are very finely ground.
>
> Beat together butter and sugar with an electric mixer until pale and fluffy, then beat in egg. Add flour mixture in 2 batches, mixing at low speed just until a dough forms. Form dough into a disk and chill, wrapped in plastic wrap, until firm, at least

2 hours.

Whisk together brown sugar, eggs, molasses, salt, and spices. Whisk in pumpkin, then cream.

Okay. That chilling part was not happening. No time.

But she could do all the other stuff.

Where the hell was the food processor?

She looked around the kitchen, but didn't see it. Shit. She checked her watch again. Then she turned back to regard the stand mixer. The damn thing had more attachments than an Electrolux. She looked them over. One of these must be used for chopping stuff.

Michael had them all arranged on a peg-board above the mixer— like medieval torture implements. Hell . . . he practically had the damn things outlined in paint.

She picked up a fat, cone-shaped and spindled metal whisk and hefted it before turning it over in her hands.

Probably this one.

She attached it to the mixer and started dumping in all of the ingredients.

All of them.

Including the flour, the brown sugar, the molasses, the solid-pack pumpkin, and the assortment of nuts and spices.

Oh . . . and the eggs. The perfectly poached eggs.

Shit.

She needed six tablespoons of unsalted butter. Softened. Well, she could go ahead and start pulsing everything else while she went and got that.

Sighing, she set the mixer control to . . . damn. There was no "pulse" setting.

Great. What the hell would be closest to that? The thing had ten speeds. Not helpful.

Okay. Let's parse it out.

She stood back and looked the unit over, critically. She'd repaired a few of these in her time. They were pretty nice machines. High-performance motors—575 watts. Planetary drive systems. Mechanical bowl lifts. Plenty of torque.

Torque had to be good for chopping. More speed equals greater torque. She set the dial to 8 and turned the unit on. It made a tortured, gurgled, grinding sound at first, but then seemed to even out. There was a dense cloud of . . . something drifting in waves up out of the bowl, but that was probably okay. It smelled sweet and spicy.

It tickled her nose.

Damn . . . that curry was really strong.

Shrugging, she walked back to the cooler to grab a stick of butter.

While she was in the cooler, she decided to go ahead and get the vegetables she'd need for the Boeuf dish, and the damn asparagus.

Let's see. Carrots. Onions. Garlic. Artichoke. Leeks.

Leeks?

Nope. Didn't need leeks.

What else?

Lard.

She forgot about that. The damn Boeuf needed to be braised in lard, not vegetable or olive oil.

Now where in the hell would he keep that? Would it be refrigerated or not?

She stood there deliberating.

Boom. Boom, boom, boom.

What the fuck? The sounds of miniature explosions continued. She exited the freezer in time to see tiny pieces of egg shrapnel flying across the kitchen.

"Oh, my god!" She ducked as a huge piece of shell ricocheted off the wall behind her.

The pan containing the eggs had boiled dry, and the eggs had blown up. Pieces of them were flying around and landing everyplace— even on the ceiling fans.

Jesus Christ.

And the stench was incredible.

Maddie dropped all the vegetables in an unceremonious heap on a prep table and ran over to the Bertazzoni to turn off the gas ring under the, now charred, All-Clad pot. Great . . . that thing was a write-off.

Pieces of egg and shell were all over the top of the stove. She didn't even want to look at the shelf behind the stove.

How would she ever get the stench out of the kitchen? And what about all that black smoke?

Wait a minute . . . black smoke?

Where in the hell was that coming from?

She stood back. Not the stove. It was off.

But the kitchen was filling up with it, and it would only be a matter of time before . . .

An ear-splitting sound cut through the air as the smoke alarm went off, and Maddie turned around to see that "Gloria" was the culprit. Dark, black smoke and flames were shooting out from the mixer's engine housing. The stainless steel whisk had been twisted into an unrecognizable shape, and finally, had stopped turning. A dense-looking, orange-colored, nut and spice magma was overflowing the bowl and dropping onto the floor in fat blobs.

She raced across the room to unplug the mixer and grabbed a towel to suffocate the flames.

"How could this possibly get any fucking worse?" she bellowed.

Ten seconds later the overhead sprinkler system kicked in, and the entire kitchen got doused in a fire-prevention monsoon.

Yeppers. This was going to be one helluva Valentine's Day.

Maddie gazed up at the ceiling with arms extended in a ludicrous pantomime of crucifixion as the overhead waterfall soaked her.

Now all she needed was for Michael to show up.

Cue Michael.

"What the fuck is going on in here? My kitchen! Oh my god . . . Gloria!"

Maddie closed her eyes.

Jesus died for somebody's sins, but not mine.

Not even Patti Smith could save her now.

Judging by the murderous look on Michael's face as he stood in the doorway to his kitchen surveying the carnage, she thanked god that she had done her residency in emergency medicine. She would've offered even money on whether or not he'd be able to kill her before he went into shock.

She was only sure of two things right now.

One. It was a very good thing that she had her attorney on speed dial.

Two. She'd never be able to mention Syd's misadventure in the hospital parking lot again.

Ever.

"I think that was just about the best meal I've ever had." Syd licked her fingertips.

37

"It was certainly the safest." Maddie poured her another glass of the cold Veuve Clicquot—the only thing she'd managed to salvage from their original dinner.

Syd stifled a laugh. "I'll say."

Maddie shoved the bottle back into its bucket of ice. "Hey, no laughing. We agreed. Truce. Right?"

"Right." Syd saluted. "Truce."

Maddie held up the big, red and white striped cardboard bucket. "Another drumstick?"

"No thanks. Four is my limit."

"Yeah. I thought you and Henry were going to have to arm-wrestle for that last one."

Syd smiled and looked at the sleeping bag in the corner of the room—still rolled out on the rug where Henry had fallen asleep after they had brought him back from Lizzy's bungalow. Maddie had long since carried him upstairs to bed, with Pete following along at her heels.

They were back at home, in their living room, lounging on the floor in front of a big fire, with the remainder of their KFC Family Feast for Four spread out on a blanket beside them.

Syd stole a glance at Maddie. Incredibly, she didn't look any the worse for wear, which was remarkable, considering the events of the evening.

By the time Syd had arrived at the inn, the fire had been contained, the sprinklers had been turned off, and Michael had been calmed down considerably by a generous dose of David's Xanax and a couple of single malt Scotches. Maddie had tried to protest the combination, but backed off right away when Michael picked up one of his waterlogged Shun paring knives and started drying it with the hem of the tablecloth.

"I'll get you some more ice," she'd said instead and beat a hasty retreat from the dining room, where they all ended up after the fire department left.

That was several hours ago, and now the unhappy chain of horrifying events was already beginning to claim its rightful place in the county annals of myth and heroic misadventure. Syd was certain that by tomorrow, no one would even remember her own fifteen minutes of fame. But Maddie's? Well. Hers could be expected to live on. For one thing, she was such an iconic figure in the lives of her patients, that any opportunity to humanize her—especially one that occurred on such a grand and epic scale—was sure to resonate with the locals for a good, long time.

But Syd had to smile as she thought about the lengths Maddie had gone to in her efforts to do something special for her, and what those efforts had nearly cost them both.

"Do I want to know what you're thinking about over there?" Maddie sounded almost tentative.

Syd gazed at Maddie. She was beautiful in the firelight. Hell. She was beautiful in any light—or in no light.

"Only how lucky we are."

Maddie snorted.

"I mean it."

Maddie still looked dubious. "It's been quite a few weeks."

Syd smiled at her. "It's been quite a year."

Maddie took her hand. "This isn't quite the evening I had planned to celebrate your birthday."

"Oh, I don't know." Syd looked around the room. "An amazing home. A beautiful fire. Great champagne. Henry." She raised their linked hands to her mouth and kissed Maddie's fingers. "You. What more could a girl ask?"

Maddie smiled. "That reminds me." She fished into the front pocket of her jeans, pulled out a tiny gold key, and held it out to Syd. "I got you something."

Puzzled, Syd took it and looked it over. "What is it?"

"It's a key," Maddie drawled.

Syd lowered it to her lap. "Thank you, Dr. Stevenson. Now that we've cleared up that mystery, would you like to tackle climate change?"

Maddie smiled. "Turn it over and look at the back."

Syd sat up straighter and held the key out toward the fireplace so she could read the tiny inscription. "429WP?"

"Right."

Syd gave her a confused look.

Maddie nudged her playfully. "Come on, blondie, reach for it."

Syd smiled as recognition dawned. "Your tail number ... of course."

"I didn't want you to forget."

Syd raised an eyebrow. "As if I could ever forget how to identify your tail."

Maddie laughed and pulled her closer. "Well ... here's hoping. But in this case, it's a functional key." She smiled. "It unlocks the airplane."

Syd dropped her head to Maddie's chest and groaned. "Like you'd ever trust me near another engine . . ."

"Oh, honey, it's just like riding a horse. You get tossed off, you get right back up on it."

"Oh, really? Think that works with KitchenAid appliances, too?"

Maddie seemed to think about that one for a moment. "Doubtful."

Syd smiled into her chest. Maddie smelled wonderful—a mix of pine and lavender.

An idea occurred to her.

"Still," she said, as she laid a trail of soft kisses along Maddie's collarbone. "I suppose we could work on that physics lesson again. I think I nearly had the hang of it last time."

"You think?" Maddie ran her hands up along the skin beneath Syd's sweater.

"Um hmmm." Syd kissed up the side of Maddie's neck. "You, know," she grasped Maddie's shoulders, "since you have that CFI rating . . ."

Maddie sighed happily. "That's CFI, MEI."

Syd kissed her chin. "Two instructor ratings?"

"Yeah." Maddie looked serious now. She lifted her head to try and capture Syd's mouth, but Syd backed away.

"Overachiever. I knew I loved you for a reason."

Maddie tried in vain to kiss her again, but Syd skillfully rolled over, and pulled Maddie along with her.

Maddie landed on top of her with a huff. "Oh, I get it now. You want some more of that hands-on instruction, don't you?"

"What tipped you off?" Syd reached a very sensitive spot and just about launched Maddie into orbit.

"Easy, baby," Maddie breathed, as she started a long, slow descent down Syd's body. "Remember. Once we hit V1, we're committed, and we have to go."

"Oh, honey," Syd tangled her fingers in Maddie's thick, dark hair, "I reached V1 ten seconds after I met you."

Like the good scientist she was, Maddie was quick to show that her own findings trended in the same direction.

And that wasn't a bad thing, for when they returned to earth, they were still wrapped up together . . . on a blanket, in front of a fire, in their own home, with the boy who would one day become their son, sleeping soundly upstairs.

Maddie's (original) Four Course Birthday Menu

Canapés au Camembert; Pancetta-Wrapped Grilled
Asparagus with Vinaigrette Dressing

Daube de Boeuf a la Saintongeaise;
Roasted Vegetables

Pan-Seared Artichoke with Balsamic Glaze

Pumpkin Custard Tart with Red-Wine
Caramel Sauce

BOTTLE ROCKET

Shawn Harris's debut novel was a runaway best seller.

In lesbian fiction parlance, a best seller was defined as any book that sold more than three thousand copies in the lifetime of its print contract. Well, Shawn's semi-autobiographical novel, Bottle Rocket, blew the lid off that equation. Within three months, her fledgling, comic romp was living up to its name and had soared right off the charts and into the annals of lesfic legend. Bottle Rocket was a bona fide hit, and Shawn was an overnight celebrity.

Nobody was more stunned by this turn of events than Shawn.

Well . . . maybe Shawn and one discriminating and outspoken reviewer for the esoteric online journal, Gilded Lily.

Kate Winston was an icon in the lesbian fiction world. Positive or negative comments from her could make or break the critical fortunes of any aspiring author brave enough to seek her approbation.

Not many dared.

Those who did and lived to talk about it went on to enjoy tremendous success and frequently acceded to the highest and most elusive level of accomplishment—crossover status.

Gilded Lily was the mainstream mouthpiece of the lesbiverse. With over 82,000 subscribers, the online magazine boasted a list of regular contributors that read like a who's who of gay culture. And Kate Winston was one of its best and most controversial bloggers.

The marketing director for Shawn's publisher never thought the likes of Kate Winston would ever look twice at the fledgling novel.

But when the sales numbers for Bottle Rocket started inching closer to the stratosphere, the editors at Lily took notice and shoved a copy of Bottle Rocket across the table toward Kate in a weekly storyboard meeting.

"We'd like you to take a gander at this book for next week," the arts and culture editor said.

Kate picked the book up like it was a piece of flotsam that had drifted her way on a red tide.

"Bottle Rocket?" she asked. She flipped it over and glanced at the blurb on the back cover. "You've got to be kidding me. I don't waste my time on pulp fiction." She dropped the book back to the table. "What else you got?"

"Kate." Linda Evans sighed. "Don't start, okay? This book is burning up the best seller lists, and we need to take a look at it."

Kate hooked a finger over the bridge of her glasses and pulled them down her nose.

"Since when do we give a shit about a book simply because it's popular? You know as well as I do that big sales numbers are usually the best indicators of indifference, not quality."

Linda wasn't in the mood to have this debate. Again. "Just humor me. Okay?"

"Why should I?" Kate crossed her arms. "I have fourteen other books already in the queue, and any one of them could paint rings around this flimsy slice of sophomoric crap."

Linda was growing exasperated. "Isn't that a bit harsh? Even for you?"

Kate shrugged.

Linda sighed. "I'll make you a deal. You review this one—without complaint—and I'll let you be the lucky dog who gets to represent the magazine at CLIT-Con in San Diego next month."

Silence fell around the room. Attending the annual CLIT-Con—an unfortunate acronym for the prestigious Creative Literary Insights and Trends Conference—was a plumb assignment. Everybody knew it. Last year, it had been in Honolulu.

Linda tried not to smile as she watched Kate fold like a cheap lawn chair.

The rest, as they say, was *herstory*.

"I have something to tell you, but you have to promise me that you won't get how you get."

Shawn dropped the phone to her shoulder and sighed. She hated it when Gwen got this dramatic. She put the phone back up to her ear.

"What is it? Just tell me, okay?"

"Nuh uh." Gwen wasn't budging. "You have to promise first."

"Good god. You act like I'm a bull in a field of spring clover."

The line was momentary silent. "And your point would be?"

Shawn stared at her computer screen and considered her options. She could hang up. But then she'd never know what prompted Gwen to call her this early on a Saturday morning. Gwen lived in Seattle, and it was barely five a.m. out there. Whatever this was about, it must be big. And bad.

Dangerous combination.

She sat back in her chair and picked up a pencil. It was a nice one—a Ticonderoga Yellow Barrel No. 2. She'd picked up ninety-six of them yesterday at Staples and spent about thirty minutes that morning sharpening them all. She didn't really write with pencils, but she liked them a lot, and felt better when she had dozens of them at the ready. You never knew . . . and it was better to be prepared.

Too bad that same prescription didn't work as well with Gwen.

She tried another approach.

"Is this about that damn podcast again? I told you I didn't want to do it. How was I supposed to know they were doing a whole segment on pleasure aids?"

"It's not about the podcast. And, by the way, you didn't help yourself by talking about the best places to shop for prostate stimulators."

Shawn felt a surge of umbrage. "Why does that one thing stick in your craw so much?"

Gwen sighed. "Maybe because your readers don't generally waste their time worrying about ways to stimulate parts they don't have?"

"I told you. I want to appeal to a broader audience."

"Trust me, Shawn, this is not the way to do it."

"Hey? I'm not without instincts here."

"That's true. And we'll get to your thoughts about the photo shoot for the AfterEllen piece later."

Shawn smelled a rat. "What's wrong with my idea?"

"Sweetie . . ."

"No. I wanna know."

Shawn could tell that Gwen was getting frustrated. She glanced at her watch. They'd only been on the phone for four-and-a-half minutes. Pretty good progress. Even for Shawn.

Gwen took a deep breath. "You'll just have to trust me on this one. No one wants to see you posing behind a soft-focused sea of chicken . . . parts."

"It's going to be tasteful," Shawn insisted. "And it's going to be shot in black and white—that's always high-toned and arty."

"Shawn . . ."

"I need a photo that speaks to the content of the book, and the narrator is a chicken sexer. It makes sense. Admit it, Gwen. Your knee-jerk response is to hate any idea I have."

Several more seconds of dead, west coast air floated across the phone line.

"Let's table the AfterEllen discussion for later," Gwen finally said. "That's not the reason I called you at such an ungodly hour."

"Okay. Why did you call me, then?"

"Gilded Lily is posting Kate Winston's review today—and they sent me an advance copy."

Shawn could hear the minor key vibrations in Gwen's voice.

"And?"

"And . . . not what we hoped for."

Shawn dropped her pencil. "She didn't like it?"

"Not exactly."

Shawn felt the junkyard dog sleeping inside her begin to stir. "What does that mean?"

"It means she hated it."

"She hated it?" Shawn was incredulous. "How is that possible? It's got sixty-three damn five-star reviews at Amazon."

"Shawn. We've talked about consumer reviews. They're entirely subjective."

"That doesn't mean they don't count."

"Of course they count, but they don't have any relationship to re-ality-based critical assessments."

"It's been in the top ten for three months—mostly at number one."

"Shawn. We talked about this. You wanted us to solicit some critical reviews, and I told you that if we did, there'd be no way to predict or to manage how they'd go."

"Well, sonofabitch."

"Relax. It's one reviewer."

Shawn snorted. "Yeah. The most important one."

"It's going to be fine. Your book is already breaking sales records for debut fiction."

"You mean, it was," Shawn grumbled.

Gwen sighed. "I'll send you this preview copy so you can read it before it posts later this morning. I wanted to be sure I had the chance to talk with you first, so you didn't go postal when you saw it."

"Yeah. Okay." Shawn indulged in a few momentary fantasies about dusting off her paintball gun and heading for SouthPark Mall. It was an idea with some merit.

Gwen was talking again. "Call me back after you've read it and had time to come down off the ceiling fan?"

"Maybe."

"Shawn?"

"Okay. Jeez, Gwen . . . I'll call you back."

Shawn's computer beeped, and a new mail flag popped on her monitor.

"Later." Gwen hung up.

Shawn leaned forward and stared at the backlighted subject line of the forwarded email.

"Simply Offal."

She sighed and dropped back against her chair. It was going to be a long, damn morning.

She wondered if she had more pencils.

244 COMMENTS. SEE ALL.

Comment from: LezBfrndz32

I can't believe you read the same book! I usually like your reviews, but this time, you really got it wrong! Bottle Rocket is a great book and your review is just rude and so are you!

Comment from: DebbieDuzGirls

Wow. It's one thing to dislike a book. It's another thing to assassinate the author! Kate Winston should be ashamed of this mean-spirited review, and Gilded Lily should never have posted it. I suggest that Ms. Winston go and read the comments from the sixty plus readers who actually understood Shawn Harris's great debut novel. Obviously, Ms. Winston missed the point.

Comment from: Westie809
Whoever checked your sex at the poultry farm tossed you into the wrong bin, chickadee! Aren't you supposed to be encouraging lesbian writers, not silencing them???? Get a new job, Kate! You're not helping.

Comment from: HellBent4Leather
Is that really you in the photo? You're hot!!!!

Comment from: HellBent4Leather
Are you on Grinder????

Comment from: CarolJ@gmail.com
I'll admit that Bottle Rocket wasn't exactly my cup of tea, but calling it "a flimsy and poorly realized faux-southern novel full of clichés, worn-out conventions, and unnecessary obfuscation" really seemed over the top. I'll agree that the premise for the novel is off-putting at first, but Harris does actually manage to make the characters real—even endearing. I wouldn't rank this book among the ten best I've ever read, but I don't agree that it's without redeeming qualities.

Comment from: AngelEyes
Ouch. Suffer from peri-menopause much?

Comment from: BillieW
Although I wouldn't have employed as much vitriol in summarizing my reactions, I would agree, in general terms, with your assessment of this book. As an author, Harris clearly has raw talent and an abundance of potential, and some of the dialogue is exceptionally bright and well crafted. But the overall premise of the novel is ridiculous and strains credibility. I think you might have over-exaggerated the negatives

here and I, for one, am anxious to see what Harris can
up with as an encore.

Comment from: HellBent4Leather
I want to play with your hair!!!

Comment from: LisaLupner
You hate everything! Why do they even ask you to read these
books? You should move over to News Corp—I hear they're
looking for some like-minded reviewers.

Comment from: FemBot
Damn Winston! I think if you pulled your head out of your ass
you might be able to get a better look at the book!

Comment from: HellBent4Leather
Oh, man. When you do this, can I watch????

Kate slammed her laptop closed and sat, shaking her head.
*Good god. I should never have agreed to read this one. I knew the
review would smoke all the Free Speech Lesbians out of their holes.*
She sighed and tapped her mouse in agitation. *Why am I so goddamn
weak? It's not like going to CLIT-Con is all that big of a deal.*

She reopened her laptop and waited for the comments page to
reload. When it finished, she noticed that something new had just
posted.

Comment from: ShawnHarris
Hello, Kate. I know we haven't been properly introduced,
but I felt the need to make some kind of acknowledgement of
your . . . review . . . of my book, Bottle Rocket. You know, I'd
like to thank you, but normally, I make women buy me dinner
before first before I allow them to . . . well . . . I think you get
my drift. Since it's clear that the nuances of my novel were
so nuanced that they managed to elude a reviewer of your
stature, maybe you'd consent to discuss the book with me
publicly, in a more balanced forum—a kind of level playing

opportunity to explain it to you in ways
vercome your apparent inability to
aning—which, by the way, I did not
ith obfuscation. Feel free to contact me
harris.com—or through our marketing
Carlisle. I think you can access her contact
ough your editor, Linda Evans? If not, let me
be happy to set something up.

Kate was incredulous.

You've got to be kidding me? Who the hell does she think she is? I'm not some junior lackey who's at the beck-and-call of an unknown, hack author.

She clicked inside the comment box beneath Harris's remarks and started typing.

Comment from: Kate Winston

Thank you, Ms. Harris, for the generous condescension. If I believed that the content of your book warranted further consideration, I certainly would take you up on your kind suggestion that we meet to discuss it. As it is, however, I think I've exhausted my quotient of interest in your fledgling foray into fiction. I wish you the best of luck with your future endeavors.

P.S. Fuck you and the horse you rode in on, honey!

Kate sat back and clicked "post" without rereading—or rethinking—her response. She knew that Linda would go ballistic when she saw this exchange, but that was nothing new. Linda went ballistic at least twice a week over something Kate did, or didn't do. This was just business as usual.

She looked again at the provocative post from Shawn Harris. It really irked her. It was so . . . arrogant.

She shook her head and closed her laptop. *Who cares?*

It was business as usual.

Right?

It was a media circus. Correction. It was a media *nightmare.*

Gwen pushed back from her laptop and thought for the thousandth time about the paltry salary she made for "managing" this kind of brouhaha. It wasn't enough. Not for Shawn. Hell, for Shawn she needed a contract rider that paid her damn hazardous duty pay.

In the three days since Kate Winston's review of Bottle Rocket posted, Shawn's public feud with the reviewer had gone viral. It was an overnight Internet sensation—a pissing contest of epic proportions. And all of the social media outlets were eating it up—even the ones Gwen hadn't heard of yet.

She looked at her computer screen.

BackDoor.com.

Just like this one. It was some kind of bizarre, fringe site devoted to profiling celebrities who were taking it up the . . . well.

Shawn was their poster child this week.

God. How was she supposed to keep up with this when it was like playing Internet whack-a-mole? The damn sites came and went faster than her string of ex-girlfriends.

And that was pretty goddamn fast.

And now, the editors at Gilded Lily were outraged because rabid fans of Shawn's had used Twitter to organize an onslaught of umbrage and crashed the magazine's website two days in a row.

How the hell was Gwen supposed to manage that?

Hell. If she figured this one out, she could give up being a marketing director for a lesbian publishing company and get Hillary Clinton's job.

To make matters worse, supporters of Kate Winston were now retaliating with a backlash of righteous indignation that made a tsunami look like a ripple in a wading pool. In the last twenty-four hours, more than sixteen toxic reviews of Bottle Rocket had been posted at Amazon.

God. These women were like pre-menstrual zealots on crack.

Gwen sighed and opened a new browser window. Might as well see what new damage has been done today.

She navigated to Amazon and pulled up the e-book listing for Bottle Rocket.

Nineteen new reviews. Great. And the overall rating had now plummeted from five stars to two and a half.

Christ.

"Where the hell are the site administrators?"

Couldn't they see what was going on here with this bullshit? Why didn't someone remove these hostile reviews?

Give that one up. Trying to find a human being at Amazon was about as useful as trying to find a virgin at a Shriner's convention.

She sat back again and picked up her coffee cup.

This was a complete clusterfuck.

She took a sip of her coffee. It was cold—of course.

Shawn was such a pain in the ass. Gwen had dozens of books to market, including five best sellers and one with a movie contract. But somehow, she seemed to spend seventy-five percent of her time dealing with Shawn.

Correction. Dealing with the messes Shawn created. Why did Bottle Rocket have to be so damn successful?

Because it's a great book.

Kate Winston plainly had some kind of burr under her saddle when she reviewed it—and whatever was biting her, it had nothing to do with the content of the novel. That much was clear. Even that servant of Cerberus over at Kirkus Reviews gave it a thumbs-up, and she never liked anything Gwen sent her way.

Nope. This was something else. And since she couldn't defuse it, it was up to her to figure out how to leverage it.

If she had a claim to fame, this was it. She was better than anyone at turning a liability into an asset. Hell. She majored in this at Wharton.

And this quagmire was one whopper of a liability.

She put down her coffee cup and picked up her cell phone.

"The best time to make hay is while the sun shines," her mentor had always said.

She scrolled through her contacts until she found the listing for the chief organizer at CLIT-Con.

The call was answered on the second ring. "Barb Davis."

Barb always sounded like she was taking bites out of the phone.

"Barb? It's Gwen Carlisle."

"Hi, Gwen. What's up?"

Gwen could hear loud banging noises in the background. Barb was a sculptor who worked with iron. It sounded like she was demolishing a Buick.

"Are you in your studio?" Gwen asked.

"Yeah. I've got a big commission for the San Diego Zoo, and I'm running behind. I'm hustling to finish this up so I can get serious about planning the Con."

"Well, you're in luck. That's why I'm calling."

The banging stopped.

"Really?"

"Yep. Have you got a topic nailed down for the plenary session yet?"

"No. I have a few suggestions, but nothing that trips my trigger." Gwen could hear the unmistakable sound of a Zippo lighter. Barb was firing up a cigarette. "Got something in mind?"

Bingo.

"In fact, I do. Have you been following the cat fight between Shawn Harris and Kate Winston?"

Barb laughed. "Who the hell hasn't been? It's getting more press than Seal stepping out on Heidi Klum."

"Sad, but true," Gwen agreed. "However, it just might make for record receipts at the Con if we think creatively."

The line was silent. She could hear Barb take another long drag on her cigarette.

"You mean, put them together on the same bill? Like a twisted Point/Counterpoint kind of thing?"

"Exactly."

More silence.

Then Barb laughed. "You're a fucking genius."

Gwen smiled. "So I've been told."

"Let me shop this idea around and get back to you."

"That'll work."

"Later." Barb hung up.

Gwen glanced down at her computer screen. During her five-minute phone call with Barb, two more hostile reviews had posted at Amazon.

She smiled.

Things were looking up.

Shawn looked at the little digital timer for what felt like the ten-millionth time.

It had to be stuck. She knew from the amount of sweat dripping off her forehead that she'd been on this damn thing for at least an hour.

She glanced at the wall-mounted TV. Kelly Ripa was gushing all over Ryan Reynolds, whose hairline was seriously starting to recede.

She hated this gym. The TVs were always tuned to horrible stuff. Didn't anybody watch the news anymore? It's not like there was a presidential election going on or anything . . . Couldn't people care about that—even a little bit?

Ten more minutes had to have passed. She glanced at timer again. Two?

No fucking way!

She hated this gym, and she hated this damn NordicTrack.

And right now, she hated Kelly Ripa, too.

Although Ryan Reynolds actually was kind of hot—in a breeder sort of way . . .

She shook her head to clear it. Okay. Clearly she'd been on this thing long enough. She was starting to get delirious.

In recent years, Shawn had been fighting a guerrilla war with her weight. Extra pounds would creep in, under the cloak of darkness, and strike without warning. Garments that once had been safe and familiar became objects of torture. And this really mattered now that she had such a public persona, and had to do so many damn interviews. She was convinced that this experience—having to squeeze her ass into "girl" clothes—was so egregious that it could replace waterboarding as a way to make even the most hardcore terrorist sing like a canary. Hell. After her first two hours in a pair of Privos, which were supposed to be casual, she was ready to confess to eighty-five capital crimes.

Gwen had taken her shopping, and they'd filled her closet with "outfits." Shawn now called this repository her WMD: Wardrobe of Mass Destruction.

She felt like a diesel mechanic in drag.

But she had to admit that Gwen knew her business, and some of that shit actually looked pretty good on her. And Gwen said that if her goal, as a serious author, was to dance to the music of the mainstream market, she had to step up and pay the piper.

On gym days, she wasn't sure it was worth the effort.

Her timer beeped. Finally. She climbed down off the machine and grabbed her towel. Cheated death again.

"Shawn? I thought that was you."

Or maybe not.

Shawn sighed and turned around to face the woman standing in front of her. Bernadette. Great.

"Hi, Bernie."

Bernadette smiled at her. Shawn could see that she was still wearing her Invisalign braces. The woman had been manic about them during the month they dated. She wouldn't eat or drink anything but water while she had them in, and she had them in a lot. Shawn thought Bernie looked . . . thin. Really thin. Kind of like a camp survivor—with unusually straight teeth. Her blonde hair was pulled back into a bun so tight that her skin was stretched across her cheekbones like Saran Wrap. She was wearing a hot pink Lululemon ensemble that looked like it had been applied with spray paint.

"Fancy meeting you here." Shawn used the end of her towel to wipe the sweat off her face.

Bernie shrugged. "I work out here all the time. I wonder why I haven't run into you before now?"

Shawn held out the front of her soggy t-shirt. "Well, as you can see, I don't." She smiled. "It's hit or miss for me, and lately, I've been missing more than I've been hitting."

"I don't know." Bernie looked her up and down. "I think you look just fine."

Shawn raised an eyebrow. There was no accounting for taste.

"And by all accounts, you're getting plenty of exercise in your online cage fight with Kate Winston."

Shawn was intrigued. "You know about that?"

Bernie laughed. "Who doesn't? It's all over Facebook. I heard that Ellen DeGeneres even Tweeted about it the other day."

Swell.

On the other hand, that couldn't be bad for book sales . . .

"For real?" Shawn asked. "What did she have to say?"

Bernie shook her head. "Beats me. But you're sure in the big leagues, now. Must be some kinda book."

"Have you read it?"

"No." Bernie slapped Shawn on the arm. "You know I'm not much of a reader, honey."

That was true. Bernadette even had a hard time making it all the way through a "Six Signs That Your Sex Life Is On The Skids" quiz in *Cosmo* without nodding off. And it was worth noting that nodding off during the quiz was one of the six signs.

"I remember," Shawn said. "Maybe you can get the audio book?"

Bernie's eyes grew round. "There's an audio book?"

Shawn rolled her eyes. "Surethere is. Meryl Streep is reading it."

"Really?" Bernie's voice dropped to a near whisper.

Shawn stared at her in amazement. "No. Not really. God, Bernadette ."

Bernie slapped her on the arm again. "You can be such an asshole. No wonder Kate Winston hates you."

"Kate Winston doesn't hate me, she hates my book."

Bernie looked incredulous. "Hello? Been to Facebook lately? Last time I checked, she had you listed in her profile under Things I Most Hate. As I recall, you were in a dead heat for third place—right after Brussels sprouts and the Tea Party."

"You've got to be kidding me?"

Bernie shook her head.

Shawn was fuming. Attacking her book was one thing, but going after her personally was a declaration of war. This bitch was going down . . . and not in any of those warm, fuzzy, I'll-call-you-in-the-morning ways, either.

She picked up her jacket and her bag. "It was great to run into you, Bernie—but I've got something I need to go and take care of." She started toward the exit, then stopped and turned back around. "How long until you get those things off?"

Bernie looked confused. "What things?"

Shawn pointed at her mouth. "Those Invisalign things."

"Oh." Bernie didn't have to think about it. "Three more weeks. Why?"

"I was thinking that maybe I could buy you something to eat."

"You mean like go out to dinner?"

Shawn shook her head. "No. Like buy you some groceries. Seriously, Bernie—you're starting to look like Karen Carpenter."

Bernie seemed horrified by the comparison. "Karen Carpenter had horse teeth."

"Yeah, well. She also digested her own organs."

Bernadette thought about that.

"Call me next month."

Shawn nodded. "It's a date."

The first thing Shawn did when she got back to her bungalow was shuck off her sweaty workout clothes. She hoped it would help to calm her ass down. Then she took a long, cold shower. She hoped that would help to calm her ass down, too. When she got out of the shower and realized that her ass was still someplace far south of calm, she opened a bottle of wine and poured herself a big glass. Why not? It was after four . . . someplace.

Maybe a few minutes on the porch with Al would help?

Shawn's house was located in a trendy, transitional neighborhood on the fringes of Dilworth—one of downtown Charlotte's more desirable residential areas. All the houses on her tree-lined street had tiny yards and big front porches. It was a nosey dog's paradise, and most of her neighbors had very nosey dogs.

Shawn's nosey dog, Al, was a big golden retriever who just showed up on her doorstep one day in the deep of summer, bearing nothing but a smile, a huge appetite, and most of a gnarled Nylabone. Shawn tried valiantly, and actually did succeed at locating Al's owners, but they said she should just keep her. They said the dog kept escaping from her run, and that they didn't really like her all that much.

Shawn didn't really want a dog, but she couldn't face turning Al over to a rescue outfit, and the Pound was out of the question. After all, she wasn't that much trouble. She seemed perfectly happy just to lounge around on Shawn's big front porch and chew on her tennis balls. And, oddly, she never tried to run off.

Shawn named her Albatross—Al for short. It seemed to fit because Al had a way of looking at Shawn with those big brown eyes that seemed to suggest she, too, knew what it felt like to carry a big load of ennui around.

They understood each other.

So Shawn sat with Al in the declining light and drank her glass of Darioush. It was fabulous. She had to admit that this was one of the best things about having a best seller—easier access to better wine.

But when even twenty minutes with a truly fine Shiraz didn't succeed in calming her ass down, she gave up and grabbed her laptop off the table next to her chair. Part of her knew that looking at Blogula's Facebook page was going to be a mistake, but she couldn't stop thinking about what Bernie told her at the gym. Hell. She might not even be able to view it.

They sure as shit weren't "friends."

She typed Kate's name into the search window, and her page loaded immediately.

Well, wrong about that.

Gwen pretty much managed Shawn's Facebook page, so she must've friended Winston, along with every other damn reviewer on the planet.

Shawn was surprised when she saw Blogula's profile photo. She was . . . interesting, in a spawn-of-Satan sort of way.

She tapped her track pad for a moment, then gave in and clicked on the icon to view Winston's photo album. A dozen small pictures filled up her computer screen. There she was, posing at some awards gala with other Gilded Lily types. She was wearing a tight little black dress with a big bow across the chest. There was another photo of her with her arms wrapped around the head of a brown and black dog. Shawn thought they kind of looked alike—both had heads full of short, husky-looking hair. No wonder some of Kate's detractors nicknamed her Eraserhead. It seemed to fit.

Cute dog, though.

Another photo showed Winston in a bikini lounging in some tropical locale.

Jeez. Why did people always cram their Facebook pages with photos of themselves looking great?

Shawn clicked on that one to make it larger.

Winston was laughing and holding onto some candy-ass-looking drink with a parasol sticking out of it. There was another woman with her in the photo. Shawn moused over her image and the tag "Randi" popped up.

Yeah. I'll just bet you were, love chunks, she thought.

So.

Eraserhead goes for the FemBot types?

It figures. No wonder she hated my book.

Shawn clicked out of the photo album.

She sat back and picked up her glass of Darioush. She really needed to spruce up her own profile photos. Not that she looked shabby or anything, but those pictures of her in Tool World posing with the 500-amp ground clamp probably didn't do a lot to make her look like a serious author. She glanced back at Kate Winston. She had dark blue eyes. Damn.

She drained her glass.

Let's get to the rat killing.

She scrolled down the page to read Winston's lists of hates and loves. How friggin' sophomoric is this?

She started to read the "loves" list. Yadda, yadda . . . poetry, yadda, yadda . . . Edgar Meyer, yadda, yadda . . . The Iron Chef, yadda, yadda . . . . Hannibal Lecter . . .

Hannibal Lecter?

She shook her head. That figures.

What else do we have here?

Under "dislikes," Winston listed bigotry, religious intolerance, Nutella, the novels of Norman Mailer, and formulaic lesbian pulp fiction. That was it. Shawn checked the list twice to see if her book—or her name—showed up anyplace. They didn't.

Bernie was nuts.

She sat back. Unless, of course, Winston considered Bottle Rocket to be an example of lesbian pulp fiction.

Probably.

She thought about that. It was true that in writing Bottle Rocket, Shawn set out to lampoon some of the more ridiculous conventions that were the mainstays of the genre—like the mind-blowing, multiple orgasms that always occurred on a first date. But she wrote that bit of apocryphal sensationalism into her book with great intentionality. It was supposed to be funny and ironic, and not a serious depiction of lesbian relationships. After all . . . everyone knew that real relationships didn't work that way. At least, they never had for Shawn.

She glanced up at Winston's profile photo again.

And probably they never have for you either, Eraserhead.

But she had to admit . . . Winston was kind of cute—in a pit bull puppy, I-know-I-look-sweet-but-I'll-rip-your-throat-out-if-you-try-to-pet-me kind of way.

A small green light in the lower right-hand corner of the page caught her eye.

Winston was online and logged into Facebook.

Before she had time to think better of it, Shawn clicked on her name and typed an instant message into the chat window.

Message from: ShawnHarris
Do you seriously think my book is lesbian pulp fiction?

A full minute went by. Then Shawn's message indicator popped up.

Winston had written back.

Message from: KateWinston
Are you talking to me?

Shawn rolled her eyes and typed back.

Message from: ShawnHarris
No. I sent this IM to Betty Friedan and it accidentally folded space and landed in your inbox. Of COURSE I'm talking to you.

It wasn't long before Winston responded.

Message from: KateWinston
It's affirming to see that you're every bit as charming as the members of your fan base.

Message from: ShawnHarris
Really? I haven't exactly seen your name on any Miss Congeniality lists. In fact, I'm fairly certain that it's YOUR claque I have to thank for all 37 of those toxic reviews at amazon.com.

Message from: KateWinston
Don't jump to conclusions. Have you considered the possibility that 37 people may have been able to claw their way past your camp followers and actually read the thing without having to down a pint of your Kool Aid first?

Shawn was incredulous. Who the fuck pissed in her Wheaties?

Message from: ShawnHarris
Want to dial it back a little bit? I'd like to think that I'm capable of recognizing and appreciating legitimate criticism when I see it.

Message from: KateWinston

All evidence to the contrary.

Message from: ShawnHarris
Hey . . . who put a nickel in you?

Message from: KateWinston
Let's see. I think you did. If memory serves, YOU contacted
ME to ask if I "seriously" thought your book was lesbian pulp
fiction.

Message from: ShawnHarris
That's true. So?

Message from: KateWinston
"So" what?

Message from: ShawnHarris
So, do you seriously think that my book is lesbian pulp
fiction?

Message from: KateWinston
Did you read my review?

Message from: ShawnHarris
Of course I did.

Message from: KateWinston
Then I'm confused about why you'd have to ask me this
question.

God. She's so infuriating.

Message from: ShawnHarris
Look. You're the one whose Facebook profile proclaims a
disdain for pulp fiction.

Message from: KateWinston
First of all, what does that have to do with you? And, second, if

you're so plainly convinced that your book is pulp fiction, then you don't need me for this conversation.

Jeez. Be a bitch, much, lady?

Message from: ShawnHarris
Look . . . I'm just trying to have an open conversation with you. Wanna stuff the rancor?

Message from: KateWinston
Sure. Wanna call off your attack dogs?

Message from: ShawnHarris
I don't happen to HAVE any attack dogs.

Message from: KateWinston
Oh, come on! They've crashed the Gilded Lily site for five days in a row now.

Message from: ShawnHarris
I am NOT responsible for the behavior of my fans.

Message from: KateWinston
Really? I don't see you out there renouncing their behavior.

Message from: ShawnHarris
And I don't see you recanting any of the vitriol you spewed about my book, either.

Message from: KateWinston
I would hardly classify my review as vitriolic.

Message from: ShawnHarris
I would hardly classify it as fair and balanced.

Message from: KateWinston
Remind me again why we're having this conversation?

Message from: ShawnHarris
Because, against my better judgment, I was hoping we could have some adult dialogue about your obvious misread of my novel.

Message from: KateWinston
It seems clear that having "adult" dialogue is a stretch for you.

Message from: ShawnHarris
I really don't understand why you feel the need to be so irascible.

Message from: KateWinston
Look. This debate is going no place. Besides, it's probably inappropriate for us to be having any kind of personal contact before the Con.

Message from: ShawnHarris
The Con?? What are you talking about?

Message from: KateWiston
CLIT-Con. You HAVE heard of it, haven't you?

Message from: ShawnHarris
Of COURSE I've heard of it. What does it have to do with this conversation?

Message from: KateWinston
Hello? We're both on the agenda for the plenary session?

What the fuck? No way! Gwen would've run something like that by me. Winston has to be blowing smoke.

Message from: ShawnHarris
I have NO idea what you're talking about. Gwen hasn't mentioned anything about that to me.

Message from: KateWinston
Really? How very singular. Barb Davis was just on the phone with my editor setting it up. But that's a moot point. I think you should hold your criticisms of my literary insights and professional methodology for our public forum in San Diego.

This was so not happening. She was going to kill Gwen.

Message from: ShawnHarris
We're going to be part of the opening session?

Message from: KateWinston
No . . . we ARE the opening session.

Message from: ShawnHarris
You and me?

If it were possible to hear someone sigh over the Internet, Shawn was pretty sure she just heard one.

Message from: KateWinston
Yes—and about 1,500 attendees.

Shawn felt like the porch floor was seizing up beneath her chair. She needed to end this conversation so she could talk with Gwen and find out what the fuck was going on. She glanced at Al, who was softly snoring on her Coolaroo. Inspiration struck.

Message from: ShawnHarris
I gotta go. My dog just ate a tennis ball.

She closed the chat window and logged out of Facebook.

Winston was gloating. That much was clear. Bitch. What a waste of skin that woman was. How dare Gwen put her in a place where she'd look so ridiculous?

Well.

To be fair, she really didn't need much help to look ridiculous. But, still. Gwen knew how Shawn was, and planning something like

64

this whole CLIT-Con gig and not telling her about it was a recipe for disaster.

Still. It would give her a chance to face Winston and hold her accountable for her rude and insidious comments about her book. And she'd get to do it in front of the audience that mattered the most. CLIT-Con was the lesbian publishing event of the year. Everyone who mattered in the field would be there.

Including representatives from the big six New York publishing houses. They were always on hand, sifting through the silt, looking for a flash in the pan.

She picked up her wine glass and smiled. Gwen knew her shit.

Yeah. This could work.

Kate was still irritated. What was with this Shawn Harris person?

It wasn't like she was a prude or anything, but she just didn't believe it was appropriate to approach people you didn't really know in all these direct and deeply personal ways. For her money, this was the biggest problem with the damn Internet. Social barriers weren't the only things that fell like Jenga blocks when Facebook went live. So did what was left of the culture's sense of propriety. Now, everyone was fair game. If you didn't like something someone said or did, you could tell them so. Directly—in real time. And you could automatically share your opinion with everyone they "knew." And everyone knew everyone these days. It was like being stuck in an endless loop with Kevin Bacon. No one was safe, and nothing had integrity.

What was that old expression? Opinions were like assholes? It was true. And today, every asshole with an opinion had instant access to a binary bully pulpit.

To hell with this.

Kate walked into her small kitchen and poured herself a glass of wine from an open bottle of Shiraz. Why not? It had to be four o'clock someplace.

That damn note from Sophie was still on the counter.

"I'd like to have Patrick next weekend," it said.

Her ex still had a key to the house, and frequently came by—unannounced—to see the dog, or to retrieve some personal item. It chapped her ass that Sophie would just breeze in and out like she still had a right to, but there wasn't much she could do about it. When Sophie left her to move into her new girlfriend's tiny loft apartment, Kate agreed to store some of her belongings until they could find a bigger place. That was nearly two years ago, and she was getting tired of having Sophie's shit still strewn around all over the house.

But Sophie did still love the dog, even if she didn't still love Kate, and Kate had a grudging respect for how attentive she remained to him. Patrick was a fuzzy, black and brown Shepherd mix with a big heart and a lopsided smile. They had adopted him from an animal rescue league not long after they bought the house in suburban Atlanta, and he quickly wormed his quiet way into both of their hearts. When their relationship fell apart, Patrick remained the one constant that led them to remain on speaking—even friendly—terms with each other. Kate often thought that he was like the Shirley Temple of dogs—a well-placed lick on the cheek and a roll of his soulful brown eyes could melt even the hardest heart—including her mother's. Even she was not immune to Patrick's full-frontal charm offensive. And on a good day, Kate's mother was like Miranda Priestly without her estrogen patch.

God. Why was she surrounded by women who seemed determined to make her life miserable? Why did she keep making the same goddamn bad relationship choices over and over? Why did her mother take such delight in pointing this unhappy trend out to her—ad infinitum? Why did this glass of wine have so many little pieces of cork floating around in it?

Goddamn it.

She set her glass down and picked up the bottle. Shit.

Where was that damn strainer?

She pulled open a deep drawer in her kitchen and looked around for it. Her Nippon sushi knives were in here—safely tucked away in their ornate wooden box. That made her think about Harris's damn book, which was set, in part, at the Zen-Nippon School for Chick Sexing in Japan.

It was a ridiculous premise, but also strangely quirky and effective. In a way, that whole Japan section of the novel worked. The prose was almost lyrical in parts, structured like intricate strands from a sequence of haiku. She'd never read anything quite like that before—certainly not in what passed for every-day, run-of-the-mill lesbian fiction.

Maybe she had been too harsh in her public assessment of the novel? It really did have some beautifully written passages.

No.

At the end of the day, it was too much like this bottle of wine—ripe with brightness and flavor, but ruined by bits and pieces of the same old crap that clogged up the entire damn genre.

Of course, she had to admit that even a compromised bottle of good wine was still drinkable, if you had the patience to strain it. Kate wasn't normally a patient person—especially when it came to her work. But wine was another matter.

She finally saw the little mesh funnel, hiding at the back of the drawer. She pulled it out and walked to a tall wooden cabinet to get a glass decanter.

Shawn Harris was somebody else's problem.

Thank god.

"Remind me again why I agreed to do this?"

They were riding in a Town Car en route back to the hotel from a book signing Shawn had just done at Obelisk—the famed GLBT bookstore in Hillcrest.

Gwen closed her eyes and rolled her head back against the plush seat. "Why didn't I spring for the limo with the minibar? You're really making me insane with this."

Shawn and Gwen had arrived in San Diego a day early so they could hold the signing event before the start of the Con. Practically since the second they met in the lobby of the Hilton Bayfront Hotel, Shawn had been second guessing her decision to attend the Con. Mostly, she had been second guessing her decision to participate in the public faceoff with Kate Winston. Shawn's alternating fits of pique, umbrage, and ennui were enough to drive Gwen to drink.

In fact, Gwen didn't really need to be driven anyplace to want to drink, but dealing with Shawn was so taxing, she was even eyeing that vegan wine they served at the hotel bar with interest.

She shook her head.

Shawn stopped her tirade long enough to notice. "What is it?"

Gwen opened an eye and looked at her.

"What are you thinking about?" Shawn asked.

Gwen shrugged. "I was thinking about vegan wine."

"Vegan wine?"

Gwen nodded.

"Seriously?" Shawn threw up her hands. "I'm pouring my heart out to you, and you're sitting there thinking about something ridiculous like vegan wine?"

Gwen nodded again.

Shawn stared back at her for a moment like she had just shape-shifted into some other kind of life form. Then she laughed. "What is that shit, anyway?"

"Beats the fuck outta me. I didn't know that wine had animal product in it."

"Well," Shawn said, "maybe it just means that the grapes aren't crushed by anything with cloven hooves."

Gwen considered that. "It certainly would add a rather nice, Old Testament flair to the product."

"I've always been a big fan of Levitical law."

"Yeah, why is that?" Gwen asked. "It seems like an odd pastime for someone named Harris."

"My mother's birth name was Muriel Abramowitz."

Gwen sighed. "Of course it was."

"By the way." Shawn nudged Gwen's arm. "Don't think I missed this flimsy attempt to distract me from my angst about this damn conference."

"How am I doing?"

"Let's see . . . that'd be someplace in the general vicinity of shitty."

Gwen rolled her eyes. "Come on. Suck it up and deal with it. You agreed, and now it's time to put on your big girl panties and face the music at this cakewalk."

"Gwen. You know I hate it when you mix metaphors like that."

"I know. That's why you write, and I handle the business. And, Shawn?"

Shawn looked at her.

"I'm goddamn good at handling the business. So please, shut up and trust me do it."

Shawn sighed and turned her head toward the window.

The car glided along Harbor Drive. It was a perfect day in San Diego. But then, every day was a perfect day in San Diego. Gwen didn't really understand why anyone would choose to live in a place without seasons. She thought about Seattle. So what if it rained two hundred days a year? At least you knew you were alive.

These collagen-stuffed people walked around like extras in a Frankie Avalon movie.

"So." Shawn was speaking again.

Gwen looked at her. "So?"

The car turned onto Park Boulevard and the hotel campus.

"Wanna go hit the bar and split a bottle of that vegan shit?"

Gwen smiled at her. "My treat."

Later that night, Shawn had some time to kill before the Pre-Con Mixer, so she wandered down to the vendor area to skulk among the tables loaded with shiny new books. She was pretty confident that no one would recognize her—she wasn't that well known in the community yet, and there was no photograph of her on her book cover. And, so far, she had resisted Gwen's insistence that she have a professional author portrait taken for general PR use. She told Gwen that she didn't want to look like a goddamn realtor.

She picked up a random book and flipped it over to view the author's photo and bio.

On the other hand . . . maybe Gwen was right. There probably was a certain advantage in not looking like you worked for Aamco Transmissions.

She took her time, winding in and out of the tables. They were piled high with titles written by the best and the brightest of the genre. All the sub-categories were represented, too. Shawn was amazed at how apparently—specific—the tastes of readers were. This was like shopping for spices at the Egyptian Bazaar in Istanbul. Every shape, size, color, and smell was represented—each promising varying degrees of zest and heat.

Shawn drifted over to a pyramid of books piled next to a hand-lettered placard that read Paranormal.

Really?

She picked one up. *The Bane of Love's Desire.*

The cover showed two well-endowed, hot women in a clinch. One of the women had very pronounced cuspids that were poised just above the carotid artery of the other.

Les-pires?

Okay . . .

She read the blurb.

> *On a desolate moonlit night, sultry heiress, Brianna Morgan, flees her engagement party to find some much-needed respite from the stresses of her impending arranged marriage to billionaire tycoon, Bryce Witherspoon. While driving aimlessly along a winding country lane, she notices a solitary figure standing at the roadside and gives in to a reckless impulse. Brianna soon discovers that Aiden, the dark and enigmatic hitchhiker, is more alluring and mysterious than anyone she's ever met before.*
>
> *Much more.*
>
> *Caught up in the erotic spell of Aiden's otherworldly hunger, Brianna discovers a depth of need and passion that she's never known before. As the two women spiral closer and closer to ultimate oblivion, Brianna is left to wonder if she is simply the next victim of Aiden's murderous bloodlust—or if together, they can overcome the curse that has held Aiden hostage for hundreds of years, and find their way to everlasting love.*

Two young women approached the table, and Shawn looked up from reading the blurb. One of them exclaimed and reached around her to grab a copy of the same book off the towering display.

"Oh my god," she cried. "Darien Black's new book is out."

Her companion snagged a copy, too.

The two women giggled and hurried off with their prizes.

Shawn shook her head and returned her copy of the book to the display.

I wonder how Kate Winston would classify this one?

At the next table was an impressive stack of books arrayed behind a label that read Mystery/Thriller. Shawn picked up a copy. *Catalina Heat.* The cover showed two well-endowed, hot women in a clinch. One of them had the barrel of a very large and shiny gun pressed against the carotid artery of the other.

She read the blurb.

> *On a hot and steamy afternoon during the dog days of August, tough and chewy butch-with-a-gun, "Cal" Callaghan,*

gets hired by the uppity Vanessa Bryson to investigate a rash of threatening emails that have been sent to her estranged daughter, the actress Miranda Somersby. There is just one condition: Cal cannot ever contact Miranda directly. But fate intervenes, and one night while Cal is driving aimlessly along a deserted coastal byway, she notices a solitary figure standing at the roadside next to a broken- down sports car. The stranded motorist turns out to be Miranda, and Cal soon discovers that there is more than one reason why Vanessa was so determined to keep the two of them apart. Cal also realizes that Miranda is more alluring and mysterious than anyone she's ever met before.

Much more.

Caught up in the glitter and fast-paced allure of Miranda's celluloid world, Cal discovers a depth of ardor and need that she's never known before. As the two women spiral closer and closer to love, the threats against Miranda escalate, plunging them both into a churning vortex of violence and unleashed passion—while Cal begins to wonder if she is simply the next unwitting stone in Vanessa's diamond-studded bracelet.

Shawn gingerly returned the book to its pile. She noticed that its author, Vivien K. O'Reilly, was scheduled to do a signing tomorrow afternoon. No wonder they had so many on hand. Shit. There had to be at least three-dozen copies of the bright orange book on the table.

She hoped that Gwen had strong-armed her boss into shipping enough copies of *Bottle Rocket* to the Con. They had high hopes for robust sales in advance of tomorrow's fireworks display at the opening session.

Better not to think too much about that right now. Her stomach was already in knots from drinking half of that weird-ass bottle of vegan wine.

She moved on to the next table.

Erotica.

Hmmmm. These books certainly had . . . intriguing cover art.

She randomly selected one. The cover showed two very well-endowed, hot women in a . . . clinch? It was hard to tell from the angle. Shawn rotated the cover. Yep. It was a clinch, all right. But wow—the detail on that leatherwork was remarkable. One of the women was holding what looked like the end of a cat-o-nine-tails against the carotid artery of the other.

She read the title. *MILF Money: Erotic Tales of Vanilla Days and Chocolate Nights* by Towanda.

Towanda? Seriously?

She flipped it over to take a gander at the blurb. Across the top, big as life, was a quote from Eraserhead herself.

> *"Move over Wisteria Lane! The only back door that sees more action than the ones belonging to these ladies is probably attached to a loading dock."* —Kate Winston, Gilded Lily

She tossed the book back to the table in disgust.

"You have got to be kidding me. And my book she hates?"

Several other shoppers standing near Shawn looked at her in surprise. Shit. She didn't mean to say that out loud. "Sorry."

She quickly left the booth and went to another table.

Historical Romance was printed in big letters on a white card.

Okay. This should be safe.

She browsed through a few of the titles, and then picked one up. *Westward Ho* by Montana Jackson. The cover showed two well-endowed, hot women in a clinch on the seat of a buckboard. One of them was wearing a cowboy hat and leather chaps, and held a knot of starched rope against the carotid artery of the other.

She read the blurb.

> *On a bleak and frigid day along the Santa Fe Trail, cattle boss Chase Cameron rescues a ragtag group of New England pioneers from a Comanche attack. Among the wanna-be settlers is sultry and independent young widow, Maris Cavanagh, who has fled her pampered Brahmin life to seek adventure on the frontier. Chase is moving her herd to Fort Dodge, and agrees to see the pioneers to safety. Early one morning during the long journey, she encounters a solitary figure standing aimlessly next to a winding stream . . .*

She placed the book back on the table.

Yeah. Okay. Checked out on this one.

The next section of books proudly reposed under a banner that read Spec Fiction.

I wonder what the hell these are about? Shawn picked up a book with a lurid cover. It showed two well-endowed, hot women, dressed in futuristic, space garb in a clinch atop some kind of metal table. One of the women was holding what looked like a hopped-up speculum against the carotid artery of the other. She read the title. *Gyno Galaxy IV: Puss and Bübs Explore Deep Spaces.*

What the hell? The author's name was V. Jay-Jay Singh.

Yeah. Shawn put the book down. I don't think so.

She took a quick look around to see if anyone was watching her. As casually as she could, she drifted over to the next table.

General/Romance.

Thank god. There were loads of books on this table. Clearly, this was one of the more popular sub-genres. One caught her eye—more because it didn't have a cover showing two well-endowed, hot women clinching anything. She picked it up. *Jericho.*

Okay. This might have potential. She turned it over to read the blurb.

> *Sultry and beautiful librarian flees carnage of a failed marriage . . . yadda, yadda, yadda . . . car breaks down . . . yadda, yadda, yadda . . . gorgeous and blue-eyed local doctor encounters a solitary figure, stranded along the side of a country road . . . yadda, yadda, yadda . . . fight their growing passion . . . yadda, yadda, yadda . . . everlasting love . . . yadda, yadda, yadda . . . on to the sequel.*

Shawn snorted in disgust and put the book down. Good god. Does anybody write anything original?

She looked back at the book. Still. I wonder how she got them to agree to that cover?

Someone bumped into her and apologized. Shawn checked her watch. The pre-Con Mixer was due to start in about twenty minutes, and the vendor area was filling up.

She heard laughter and looked toward the coppery sound. Three women were standing together near a big table loaded with hats and koozies—all emblazoned with CLIT-Con logos. One of the women caught Shawn's eye. She was on the short side, with a head of cropped, gray-streaked, husky-looking hair—the kind you just wanted to play with. She was still laughing at something someone had said, and she had a fantastic set of dimples. The rest of her assets looked pretty appealing, too.

Shawn stood there, trying to persuade herself that she really did need a ten-thousandth koozie, when someone behind her called out to the group.

"Kate! What time did you get here, babe?"

A very large woman, wearing a tight black Harley t-shirt that proclaimed, "If you can read this, the bitch fell off," pushed past her and made a beeline for the group. She had an impressive mullet that fell below her broad shoulders.

She wrapped the smaller woman up in a big, butchy bear hug, and then turned around to motion another woman over.

"Greta? Get over here and meet the famous Kate Winston."

Shawn was stunned. Every ounce of that shitty vegan wine started to bubble up inside her.

Ohmygod. Did I really almost go over there and hit on fucking Eraserhead? How did I not recognize her? It must have been the glasses . . .

She needed to hide. She needed to throw up.

She needed to find a goddamn exit sign.

This was not happening. In her haste to escape, she backed into a tall pyramid of books and knocked it over. Of course, it would be the biggest fucking display in the whole fucking vendor area of the whole fucking conference. And of course, every fucking person in the whole fucking hall turned around to fucking stare at the fucking klutz who fucking knocked it over. Including She of the Poison Pen.

Shawn got to her knees and scooped up the books.

Oh god. The display contained about twelve thousand copies of *Gyno Galaxy IV*. Wait. That wasn't all. There also were copies of *Gyno Galaxy II*, *Gyno Galaxy III*, and the flagship of the series, *Gyno Galaxy: Probing Explorations.* Good god.

On the other hand . . . V. Jay-Jay had an entire Gyno *franchise?*

She needed to talk to her publisher . . .

The pre-con mixer was rocking and rolling. Literally This year, the organizers were basking in receipts from record-breaking registration numbers. This meant that in addition to better (non-vegan) wine that actually came in bottles, and cheeses imported from places more exotic than Indiana, there was music. Live music. Played by live musicians, with real instruments. And they were actually good—unlike last year's endless, canned recordings of Israel Kamakawiwo'ole.

However, Kate did have to admit that his cover of "Sisters are Doin' It for Themselves" was surprisingly tuneful and upbeat. Who knew you could riff on a ukulele like that?

She had staked out a nice corner behind one of the huge potted palms near the wine bar, and was doing her best to avoid getting sucked into conversations with . . . well, anyone. She was on sensory overload from having to listen to so many endless appeals for reviews, and just wanted to enjoy a few minutes of solitude. She put on her reading glasses and did a halfway credible job of hiding her nametag beneath her jacket, in the hopes that most people wouldn't recognize her. So far, it seemed to be working pretty well.

What she really wanted to avoid was running into Shawn Harris—who was certain to be here tonight.

She scanned the big ballroom again.

Not that she'd even know how to recognize Harris if she did show up. The photo on her Facebook page didn't reveal much. The author was wearing a red ball cap that covered most of her face, and there was no photo on her book jacket. Her Web page had the same damn hat picture—Harris was obviously very attached to that tool thingy she was holding. Ridiculous. Why would her publisher put up with that kind of sophomoric crap?

Kate drained her second glass of wine and wondered how long she'd have to wait for the crowd near the bar to thin out so she could mosey over and ask that surly bartender for a refill. What was his problem? It wasn't like he was paying for the stuff himself.

Maybe he just didn't like lesbians?

She smiled. If so, he was in for a long night.

She thought about Harris's book again, and their artfully choreographed, *High Noon*-stylefaceoff tomorrow afternoon.

If you held her down and threatened her with death, dismemberment, or sharing an elevator with Newt Gingrich, she'd have to admit that some parts of *Bottle Rocket* hinted at a quirky kind of originality. And it was also true that there were occasional snatches of prose that weren't half bad ... once you got past the overblown language and epic conventions.

God ... what was with the crush of people just standing there near the damn bar? The surly bartender caught her eye. I know you're going to make me open another bottle of the Shiraz, his gaze seemed to say.

Kate looked away and tried to hide her empty wine glass.

Shit. She saw Quinn heading her way. The big woman was still wearing her black Harley shirt and a tight pair of jeans that were several sizes too small. For some reason, she had added a pair of zip-on leather chaps to her ensemble, and they made her legs look like overstuffed sausages.

"Kate?" The voice came out of nowhere and scared the shit out of her. She jumped, and nearly dropped her glass. It was Gwen Carlisle.

"Since when did you become one of the Con Palm-Pilots?" Gwen asked. "What are you doing hiding out back here?"

Kate smiled with relief. "Gwen. Thank god you're here." She lowered her voice. "Right now, I'm hiding from Quinn."

Gwen looked confused. "Quinn? Quinn who?"

"Quinn Glatfelter."

Gwen looked incredulous. "The BDSM author?"

"That's the one."

"She's here?" Gwen glanced around.

Kate grabbed her by the arm. "Stop it. She's right behind you."

Gwen turned back toward her. "Was that her in the chaps?"

Kate nodded. "Yeah. Subtle. Kinda hard to miss, isn't she?"

"I'll say."

Kate couldn't tell if Gwen was appalled or intrigued.

"Is your publisher interested in broadening their author list?" She paused. "Literally?"

Gwen snorted. "Very funny." She took a big sip from her tall pilsner glass. Funny. Kate would never have pegged Gwen as a beer drinker. "Tell me, Kate. Why aren't you a writer? We'd sign you in a heartbeat."

"I am a writer." She raised an eyebrow. "I think it's possible that you might have a passing familiarity with some of my recent prose work?"

"That's not what I meant, and you know it. But while we're on the subject. Why did you eviscerate Shawn's book the way you did? You know as well as I do that it's a great read. Exponentially better, I'll warrant, than seventy-five percent of the crap that crosses your desk."

Kate shrugged. "That's true."

"So? Why the hatchet job?"

Kate looked at her. "You think Harris has the chops to make it as a mainstream novelist, don't you?"

Gwen nodded. "Of course I do."

"Well. So do I."

Gwen's jaw dropped. "Excuse me?"

"You heard me."

"Oh, I heard you all right. I just don't understand you. Why the hell would you post a toxic review like that of a book you really liked?"

"I didn't say that I liked *Bottle Rocket*. I said that I agreed with you that Shawn Harris has the chops to make it as a mainstream author. This book, however, is not the vehicle that will get her there. Any shot at real brilliance it had was completely undercut by its regrettable adherence to the same old clichés and worn-out plot devices that define most of the genre."

Gwen stood there for a moment without speaking. "It's hard to argue with you, Kate. You know your shit."

Kate was unfazed by the compliment. "That's what they pay me for."

"Still," Gwen continued, "you have to admit that *Bottle Rocket*, as a lesbian novel, deserved higher marks than you gave it."

Kate shrugged. "I don't rank books according to how much better or worse they are than the rest of what's floating around in the shallow end of the pool. I'm a critic, not a reviewer. There's a difference."

"Care to explain the difference to me?"

"I'd be happy to," Kate smiled sweetly at her, "tomorrow at ten o'clock."

Gwen sighed and finished her beer. "You're a tough nut to crack, Winston."

Kate did not disagree. "So they tell me."

Gwen held up her pilsner glass. "I'm dry. Wanna stroll on over to the bar and get topped off?"

Kate hesitated.

"Oh, come on." Gwen took her by the elbow and tugged her forward. "This damn plant isn't going anyplace."

They walked toward the bar. The line was ridiculously long. She noticed that most of the people in the line were holding two glasses—

one empty, and one someplace short of empty. Smart. It seemed like a good system—top them both off, then rotate back around to the end of the line and start all over again.

She sighed. "We're going to be here all night."

"Nah," Gwen reassured her. "It's all in who you know."

Kate looked at her. "What do you mean?"

Gwen held up a forefinger. "Watch and learn." She scanned the line ahead of them. "Vivien!"

A small, redhead, wearing a lime green jumpsuit, turned around, then waved vigorously when she saw Gwen.

"I heard from the Poughkeepsie Public Library," Gwen called out.

Vivien waved them both forward. "Come on up here with us," she shouted over the din.

Gwen nudged Kate. "See? Told you."

They advanced two-thirds of the way forward in the line.

"Viv, meet Kate Winston."

Vivien K. O'Reilly trained a pair of very round and surprised eyes on Kate.

"No shit?" She looked Kate over. "The She-Bitch herself. Badass hair."

"Um . . . thanks?" Kate replied.

Gwen chuckled. "So, Viv. The Poughkeepsie Public Library would love to have you do a reading—and we can fit it in right before the Rehoboth shindig."

"Fabulous." Vivien did a little joyous jig and waved the hand holding her pilsner glass around. A spray of white foam flew all over the back of the woman standing in line just front of her. Fortunately for Viv, she was too engrossed in her conversation with V. Jay-Jay Singh to notice.

V. Jay-Jay Singh?

Oh shit.

V. Jay-Jay had been after Kate for months to review her Gyno Galaxy series, and Kate had dodged or ignored so many calls from her that she'd need an abacus to count them all. She looked wistfully at her potted palm, then down at her empty wine glass. It was a tough call—more wine, or facing the music with V. Jay-Jay.

Someone walked past them, carrying two wine glasses that had plastic tops.

Go cups? For real?

Kate touched Gwen on the sleeve. "Excuse me, I think I may have

78

left the iron on in my room. I'm gonna duck out and go check on it, okay?"

"Gwen looked at her strangely. "Okaaaaay."

Kate held out a hand. "Nice to have met you, Viv. Best of luck with your book."

"Thanks." Viv shook her hand and gave it a little squeeze before releasing it. "I wasn't kidding about the hair."

"Really?" Kate raised an eyebrow. "How about the 'She Bitch' part?"

Viv thought about it. "No. I pretty much meant that, too. But from me, that's not a bad thing." She looked Kate up and down again. "Not bad at all."

Kate gave her a wary little smile and walked off, wondering for a moment if Viv might actually be the elusive HellBent4Leather character who now made regular appearances on her blog.

She fought an impulse to run a hand through her short, husky hair. What was so damn odd about it?

She walked toward the main doors to the lobby and its bank of elevators and saw yet another crush of people she needed to maneuver around. It felt like a damn conspiracy. Every person she'd pissed off or worked to avoid for the last five years seemed to be attending this conference en masse.

She veered off and doubled back toward the wine bar, where Gwen and Viv were no longer in evidence. They must've refilled their glasses and headed off for greener pastures. A makeshift bussing area had been set up behind the bar, and beyond that was a door that probably led to the service galley for this ballroom. White-coated servers buzzed in and out, carrying large trays of hors d'oeuvres and crates of glasses. Maybe I can sneak through there and make my way back to the elevators without being noticed?

As she got closer to the service area, she realized she wasn't the only one to have this idea. Another woman was lounging around back there, doing a poor job of acting like she belonged in that part of the reception area. Kate could tell by the way she kept stealing nervous-looking glances around the room as she inched closer to the exit that she didn't quite have the confidence required to sneak out with authority.

Amateur, she thought.

A server, carrying a big tray of dirty plates and glasses, nearly knocked the woman over as he flew past her en route to the galley. Kate laughed as the woman comically jumped out of his way, then quickly looked around to see if anyone had noticed. She saw Kate looking back at her and turned five shades of red. She quickly cast about like the room was on fire, and she was desperate to escape.

Kate thought she was cute, in a clumsy Ellen DeGeneres-meets-Buster Keaton sort of way. She had wispy hair with blonde highlights, and smiling eyes—even though they looked panicked and a bit maniacal right now. She was wearing faded jeans, a white blouse with an oversized man's tuxedo jacket, and running shoes that looked like they'd seen a lot of hard use. She wasn't petite, but she wasn't large either. She just looked . . . solid. Like someone you could tuck into and not worry about toppling over. Like someone who might still be standing after being hit by a tsunami, or a horde of impatient busboys.

The woman stole another look at Kate, and her agitation seemed to increase.

Kate decided to take pity on the poor creature and scout around for another way to escape the mixer. She turned on her heel to head toward the main lobby exits and ran smack into a tall busser carrying a big tray loaded with empty . . . somethings, who was making a beeline for the back of the hall. He was more fleet of foot than Kate, and managed to dodge her without spilling his cargo—a feat that earned him a hearty round of applause and a few wolf whistles from the revelers who were close enough to witness the near disaster.

Kate didn't fare quite as well.

She went sprawling into a cluster of big potted plants that had been concealing another group of shy types. When she exploded through the leafy wall of their hideout, they scattered like beads from a broken necklace. In her clumsy attempt to right herself and minimize her mortification, she slipped on a big clump of Spanish moss. She lost her footing again—this time, crashing into a table where several authors were seated.

Miraculously, they all managed to pick their drinks up off the table before Kate came to rest on top of it.

"Well," she heard one of the authors remark, as she lay spread-eagled across their plates of canapés and crudités, "this has to be the best damn hot bar I've ever had at one of these things."

Kate rolled her head toward the sound and realized two things—the side of her face was now covered with something pasty that tasted like pretty good pimento cheese, and the voice above her belonged to none other than V. Jay-Jay Singh.

Life was a capricious bitch, and she took no prisoners.

Well, she thought, morosely. *At least I created enough of a diversion to allow that other poor schmoe to escape.*

The other poor schmoe didn't waste any time beating a hasty retreat, once all eyes in the room were pointed toward the spectacle of the miraculous, tumbling blogger.

Shawn smiled. If Kate Winston weren't such a complete virago, she'd actually feel a little sorry for her. It had to be mortifying to end up flat on your back like that—splayed out across all those little plates like the world's biggest appetizer. And what a drag to take a tumble and end up in a supine position on top of the table belonging to the erotic authors.

On the other hand, it couldn't happen to a more deserving subject.

Still. Eraserhead did look kind of cute with all those bits of kale sticking out of her hair . . .

Shawn punched the elevator button for the ninth floor.

She still needed to finish her opening remarks about Bottle Rocket for the faceoff tomorrow. The moderator asked her to prepare a short, two-minute intro that would bring the audience up to speed about the plot and themes of the book. She'd been trying to work on it in fits all day and wasn't making much progress. Probably because she knew that Winston was doing her version of the same thing, and she felt hamstringed, trying to second guess what the acerbic critic was likely to say.

For some reason, the damn elevator was stopping on every floor. Each time it came to rest, the doors would roll back, but no one would be standing there. Shawn kept pushing the button with the big, illuminated number nine on it, but the thing just took its sweet time. She glanced up at the brass plate fastened above the door opening. Otis. It figured. Her Uncle Warren used to work for the old Otis Elevator Company in Erie, and she recalled that he always moved in the same deliberate way, no matter how much Aunt Jane yelled at him to hurry up.

She pulled a folded piece of paper out of her jacket pocket and looked it over. Lame. Her remarks were nowhere near pithy enough to counter the slash-and-burn summary that she was positive Kate

Winston would be delivering to the salivating crowd tomorrow. She shoved the paper back into her pocket without bothering to refold it.

The elevator groaned and stopped again. Fourth floor. Shawn waited for the big metal doors to roll back. They did. And, once again, there was nothing waiting out there but a big swath of hideous carpet. What was that pattern, anyway? Cabbage roses?

Maybe I should just get off and take the damn stairs.

She was too agitated. Acting like a total klutz in front of Winston all but obliterated the tiny bit of chutzpah she had left. She tried to imagine what proverbial bit of wisdom her mother would reel off right now—after she exhausted her usual litany of complaints.

> *"How long has it been since you got a haircut?"*
> *"Those pants make you look like you're standing in a hole!"*
> *"Why don't you wear some makeup? You look like death takes a holiday."*
> *"Are you still seeing that blond bimbo with the braces?"*
> *"Why can't you settle down with a nice boy like your cousin, Jerome?"*

It always took her a while to get warmed up.

> *"Don't be so mishugina—this, too, shall pass. You worry too much, Shawnala."*

That part was certainly true.

She looked down at her shoes.

Her mother might be right about the pants, too.

Shawn sighed. Maybe a good workout would make her feel better. There was nothing quite like working up a good sweat to get her mind off the other things in her life that were making her crazy.

The elevator stopped again. Fifth floor.

Seriously?

On the other hand, why worry? By the time she reached the ninth floor, the fucking conference would be over.

She leaned back against the wall of the tiny metal box and resolved just to enjoy the ride.

Sometimes, things just had a way of working out the way they were supposed to.

The shower didn't make her feel much better. But she knew it would take more than a damn shower to take the edge off her grand departure from the conference room trailing bits of wilted lettuce and crushed mini-quiche in her wake—not to mention the bright orange swath of cheese spread that was plastered to her hair like spackling compound.

It was not a good look. And it didn't help that it was V. Jay-Jay Singh who hauled Kate to her feet and brushed the worst of the . . . comestibles from her clothing. And Kate didn't miss the fact that V. Jay-Jay managed to work in a gratuitous grope of her backside while she was "helping" her out.

Erotic authors. Jesus, Mary, and Winston Churchill on a cracker. Why did it have to be their table she chose for her Flying Wallenda act?

How in the hell was she supposed to stand up in front of all these people tomorrow and put her best Bitch on, now that they'd all seen her splayed out like some kind of ludicrous Blue Plate Special? Her only consolation was that maybe Shawn Harris hadn't been in the room to witness it. That would have been the final mortification—the last nail in the coffin containing what was left of her self-confidence.

Shit. This was getting her no place. She'd never be able to relax and get any sleep.

She picked up the fat notebook that contained the roster of hotel amenities and flipped through its laminated pages. There was a decent-looking fitness center on the concierge level. Maybe forty-five minutes on a treadmill would clear her head?

It was nearly nine-thirty. She had just over twelve hours until the opening session's battle royal with Shawn Harris commenced. She needed to find a way to unwind, or she'd be worthless tomorrow. And working up a good sweat always did the trick.

Why not give it a shot?

She changed into shorts and a t-shirt and snapped up her card key. Nobody would be in the workout room at this hour. She left her room and headed for the bank of elevators at the end of the hall.

She ought to be safe.

Kate got to the fitness center and was greeted by a couple of annoying discoveries: she was not alone, and one of the four workout machines was in obvious disrepair. A placard taped to the front of the broken unit proclaimed that it would be repaired by . . . Kate squinted to read the date. *Three weeks ago?*

She sighed and rolled her eyes.

Of course, the two other hotel guests who had picked this ungodly hour of the night to work out had installed themselves on the functioning end units, leaving only the middle right treadmill between them available. They were both running. At least, the woman was running. The large man with a very hairy back and spandex shorts that left little to the imagination, was doing more sweating than anything.

She looked around for alternatives.

There was a wall-mounted flat panel, tuned to HGTV, or "Hey Girl TV"—an odd choice for a workout room. Beneath it, a sagging rack held up an indifferent-looking set of hand weights. It was tucked next to a long bench covered with ripped red vinyl.

It was a conundrum. The weight bench or the center treadmill were her only options. She looked at the weights again.

Don't see that happening.

She was too embarrassed to turn around and leave, so she dropped her bag to the floor and resolved to try a twenty-minute run on the center treadmill. That was long enough to be respectable, and maybe she'd luck out, and the other two people would finish up and leave so she could enjoy some solitude.

The large, hairy man was grunting now and shaking his head with apparent disgust at the hideous padded headboard that designer David Bromstad had just added to someone's Florida vacation home. Everyone's a critic. But, in fact, Kate did not disagree with him. The monolithic headboard was hideous enough to adorn a high-roller suite at the Bellagio.

As discretely as she could, she took her place on the center machine. The woman to her right glanced at her, then quickly looked away as if she'd seen a ghost.

What is her problem? She programmed her unit, and the rubber conveyor beneath her feet moved. Soon, the three runners were laced into their individual rhythms, and the only sound in the small room came from the slapping of their shoes against the mechanical moving sidewalks.

Meanwhile, David Bromstad had completed his appointments in the master suite of the house he was making over. The result was too much for the man in the spandex shorts. With a snort, he punched the stop button on his treadmill and grabbed his towel.

"That looks like a goddamn bordello," he said to no one in particular. "This dude should be designing Motel 6 lobbies." He climbed down off his machine and huffed his way out of the room

Kate just shrugged and kept running. The woman beside her didn't even look his way. She was too intent on staring at something fascinating on the blank wall next to her treadmill. The two of them ran on in silence for a few more minutes until they fell into step with each other. Their footfalls seemed to strike the conveyors with exactly the same cadence. It was eerie, and began to feel awkward to Kate. As discretely as she could, she reached out and punched up the speed on her machine. That was better. She was running faster now.

Then the woman beside her did the same thing. After a few seconds, they were running in tandem again.

Are you kidding me with this?

Kate reached out and punched the up arrow. Two clicks this time. In short order, the woman beside her caught up again.

Kate was incredulous. *What the fuck?*

She punched her up arrow three more times. She was edging dangerously close to the unit's top speed, but damn if she'd let this annoying woman best her. It wasn't long before the other woman followed suit. They were both flying now. It was ridiculous. The muscles in her legs were starting to sing from the exertion. This was really far too fast for her, and she knew there was no way she could sustain this pace for very long. Her machine whined—it sounded like the bearings were shot.

Great.

She was starting to sweat now—profusely. But damn if she'd be the one to slow down first.

The run went on and on. Well past good sense or safety. David Bromstad morphed into Candice Olson. Now, someone's kitchen was getting the Motel 6 makeover.

Beside her, the woman with the short blond hair was panting. Hard.

Serves you right, Kate thought. Her shirt was so soaked with sweat it was sticking to her like a second skin. It was getting harder to remain coherent. She was feeling light-headed. Not a good sign. She needed to slow down before she passed out.

She heard an odd, thumping sound. At first, she thought it was part of the motor whine coming from her treadmill—the thing sounded like it was on its last legs. But then she realized the sound was tied to her foot striking the rubber conveyor. She glanced down. Shit! The entire sole of her shoe was flapping like the loose jaws of that woman who had been ahead of her in the drink line at the Pre-Con mixer.

Nice. So much for these damn hundred-and-fifty-dollar Gel Kayanos.

Now she'd have to stop, or risk tripping over her sole.

What a cruel pun. Even Kate had to smile at the irony of that one.

Just as she reached out in defeat to slow her machine down, the bottom of her shoe flew completely off, breaking her stride. She stopped running and started stumbling, but the conveyor kept moving at its programmed, breakneck speed. She was airborne for the second time that night with no admiring coterie of erotic authors to break her fall. She was going down. Hard.

"Fuck me!" she yelled, as she spun completely around and fell toward the unmoving treadmill that had been vacated by hairy-back spandex-man. She flailed her arms like a lunatic, pirouetted, and finally came to rest flat on her back. As she fell, the yawning abyss of the rest of her life unreeled before her eyes in cold and unforgiving black and white—a bleak and relentless film montage that made the best of Ingmar Bergman look like a Mel Brooks double feature. She'd be a paraplegic—living a somber and colorless life of abject solitude in someplace hideous like . . . Indiana, routinely spewing her pent-up vitriol by writing caustic, unsolicited reviews with a breath-controlled mouse.

Roll credits. Cue the orchestra. Bring up the house lights.

While Kate was busy watching her personal home movie, her companion hit the emergency stop button on both machines and scrambled over to her.

"Good god!" she gasped. She was still breathing heavily from her own ridiculous part in their duel with disaster. "Are you okay?"

Kate's legs were sprawled across her own treadmill at an impossible angle. One foot was still caught beneath the conveyor of the unit by what was left of her mangled shoe.

"Do I look okay?" she hissed, before she could think better of it.

"Sorry," she added.

"It's okay." The other woman knelt beside her. "Can you sit up?"

"I think so." Kate allowed the woman to slip an arm behind her shoulders and help raise her into a sitting position. Her heart was still pounding from the aftermath of her run and the adrenaline rush that accompanied her dismount.

"Let's get your foot out from beneath that conveyor," she said. "Can you move it?"

"I'm afraid to try," Kate said. "My ankle hurts like hell."

The woman nodded. "It's already swelling. You'll be lucky if it's not sprained."

"You think?" Kate grimaced as the woman carefully extracted her foot from beneath the belt. "I knew I overpaid for these damn shoes."

"I think we should get this off your foot—in case your foot starts to swell, too."

"It won't swell," Kate deadpanned. "You only get that feature if you spring for the pumped-up kicks."

"Better run, better run?" The blonde woman unlaced Kate's mangled shoe. Kate looked up at her with interest. She had hazel eyes that were crisscrossed with smile lines.

Kate nodded. "Faster than my bullet."

"Interesting metaphor." The woman dropped Kate's shoe to the floor. "You like Indie bands?"

"Not really," Kate replied. "But I've done my time at outdoor music festivals."

"Groupie?"

Kate rolled her eyes. "Hardly. I used to be a stringer for Wired."

"Really?" The other woman looked intrigued. "Why'd you give that up?"

"Ever been to Manchester, Tennessee in June?"

The woman thought about it. "Bonnaroo?"

Kate nodded. "Sharing a bathing trough with fifty-thousand stoners tends to lose its magic after the first few visits."

"I don't know. That sounds a whole lot like my fond memories of scout camp."

Kate raised an eyebrow.

"We were an esoteric group. We earned badges for things like converting smudge pots into bongs."

Kate narrowed her eyes. "Did you say scout camp? Are you sure you didn't mean to say Wilderness camp?"

The other woman shrugged. "You say tomato . . . Besides." She waved a hand. "What's the difference, really?"

Kate rubbed her sore ankle. "For starters, a juvie probation officer and a court order."

The other woman laughed. She had a great smile. "Spoken like someone familiar with the drill."

"I had two older brothers," Kate explained. "Let's just say that I barely escaped deportation."

The blonde was still smiling. Kate thought that something about her seemed familiar, but she couldn't quite place it. She really was awfully cute. Kate wondered if she were in San Diego for the Con. There were reputed to be upwards of six hundred lesbians staying in this hotel. It would be just her luck to stumble across one of the straight ones.

Literally.

"Think you can stand up?" The woman gestured at Kate's sore ankle.

Kate sighed. "Only one way to find out."

"Can I give you a hand?"

Kate hesitated for only a second. "Sure. If you don't, I'll probably have to spend the night in here, watching reruns of bad headboards."

The other woman stood up and offered Kate her arm. "I think that might actually violate the Constitutional ban on cruel and unusual punishment."

"Don't believe it." Kate took hold of her arm and slowly hauled herself to her feet. "They said the same thing about Ice Capades." Her ankle hurt like hell, but she actually was able to put a bit of weight on it without screaming. It could have been a lot worse, and with her, it usually was. Maybe things were looking up.

"How's that feel?"

Kate turned her head to look at the other woman. Their faces were very close together.

Yep. Things were definitely looking up.

"It's not as bad as I was expecting," Kate said.

"Think you can walk back to your room?" the woman asked. "Or is there someone I can call for you?"

"No," Kate said a bit too quickly. "I'm here alone."

Oh . . . smooth, Winston, she thought. Why don't you just offer her your goddamn room key?

She tried to cover her mortification. "I'm here for the literary conference."

The woman nodded. "Me, too."

Score.

"Really?" Kate tried to feign innocence as they slowly walked toward the red weight bench so she could sit down. Who the hell was she? Was she here with anyone? And more importantly, had she been downstairs when Kate took her first nosedive of the evening?

She sat down. "What do you do?"

The woman let go of her arm and stepped back. She looked embarrassed. "I'm . . . one of the . . . um . . . authors."

Kate was surprised. "You are? What genre?" No wonder she looked familiar.

"Um. I don't really fit any of the standard categories."

Kate was intrigued. "You don't? What have you written?"

The woman shrugged.

Kate thought her coyness was charming. "Tell me. If it's one of the books being featured at this Con, I've probably already read it."

The woman seemed extremely uncomfortable now. She was looking anyplace but at Kate.

"Yeah, I know," she finally said. Then she sighed. "What the hell?" She looked at Kate. "You have read my book. And tomorrow morning at ten o'clock, you're going to tell me and half the population of the lesbiverse why you hated it so much."

Kate felt all the blood drain from her face. This was not happening. She closed her eyes. "You're Shawn Harris."

It was not a question.

The author of *Bottle Rocket* nodded. "Guilty."

Kate's head throbbed in sync with her ankle. "You know," she said in a small voice, "maybe I will just stay here tonight."

"You really don't have to do this," Kate said for the tenth time through clenched teeth, as she limped along a boulevard of rust and amber curlicues toward her room. Who designs these fucking carpets? She winced as they turned a corner. Probably that Motel 6 guy. They still had another long hallway to traverse. Kate had been adamant about getting a room as far away from the elevators as possible. These conferences were like key clubs, and she didn't want to be up half the night listening to the damn doors open and close.

"Of course I do," Shawn Harris said sweetly for the tenth time. "Sometimes, adhering to conventions is a good thing."

Kate grimaced, and not because of her ankle. "I never said your book was conventional."

"You didn't?" Harris asked. "I'm pretty sure you said it was 'full of clichés and worn out conventions.'" She looked at Kate. "I guess that's not the same thing?"

Kate was getting pissed off. She wanted nothing more than to be back in her room—alone—and away from this annoying woman. "It's not the same thing, and you know it as well as I do."

"Oh, really? Care to enlighten me?"

Kate glared at her. "I don't think Mother Teresa could enlighten you. Why the hell should I try?" She tried to pull her arm away, but Shawn held on.

"Now, now. Don't be stupid. You need to hang on to me until we reach your room, or you'll fall flat on your cute little ass." She squeezed her arm. "Again."

Kate was furious with her. "You're really enjoying this, aren't you?"

"Let's see . . ." Shawn looked like she was pretending to think about it. "Yeah. I am."

"Fine. Let's have it your way. I'd be happy to tell you exactly what I thought about your debut novel."

"Too little, too late, Winston. You've already shared your unique perspective with me, and with about eighty-thousand of your closest friends."

Kate shook her head. "You're not hearing me. I said I'd tell you what I thought—not what the critic paid by Gilded Lily thought."

Shawn looked at her. "There's a difference?"

Kate rolled her eyes. "Of course there's a difference."

They walked along in silence for a moment.

"Color me so confused," Shawn said.

Kate limped along without speaking.

Shawn tried again.

"Or if you don't want to do that, you can always just *Color Me Barbra*."

Kate looked at her with a raised eyebrow.

"Hey, it was a seminal recording," Shawn explained. "In my house, your choices were Barbra Streisand or the best of Fred Waring and The Pennsylvanians. Believe me, it wasn't pretty."

Against her will, Kate laughed.

"Imagine my complete confusion when they moved me to North Carolina at age twelve. Now you know why I escaped to Japan. It was about as far as I could go without ending up back where I started."

Kate was surprised. "You really did that?"

"Really did what?"

"You really went to Japan?"

"Of course I did."

Kate was silent.

"What did you think? That I just got all that shit off Wikipedia?"

Kate didn't respond.

Shawn shook her head in amazement. "That's what you thought, isn't it? That I just pulled that stuff outta my ass."

"No, that's not what I thought. In fact, I thought the whole Japan section of your book was beautifully written. Authentic. Almost transcendent in its originality."

Shawn stared at her stunned. "Then why the fuck didn't you say that?"

"Because it's not my job to jack-off new authors who are drinking their own Kool Aid. Your fans were already canonizing you, and it was clear that you were well on your way to a more mainstream market. In my view, you needed to take a few body blows to toughen you up before you jumped headfirst into the big leagues."

Shawn looked incredulous. "Just who the hell do you think you are. Some twisted, Internet incarnation of Albert Schweitzer? Trust me. Your brand of help I could do without."

"Oh, please. You thought I was hard on you? You wait until the *New York Times Book Review* sinks its teeth into your pampered little ego. Mark my words—if you crank out another novel that caves in to the same worn-out, hackneyed conventions we've all read a zillion times, the best you can ever hope for will be competing for space in the remainder bin at Books-A-Million."

Shawn didn't reply, but Kate could tell that she was fuming. A band of red was slowly making its way up her neck, rising above the collar of her gray t-shirt. Kate came to an abrupt halt in front of a door.

"This is me."

Shawn let go of her arm. "It sure is."

Kate fumbled in the pocket of her shorts for her key card. In a few more seconds, she'd be safe and alone in her room, and the events of this evening would just be a bad memory. Correction. Another bad memory. She seemed to be racking them up with gusto these days.

"Thanks for the help," she said without emotion.

Shawn shrugged. "Wish I could say the same."

Kate sighed. "I guess I'll see you tomorrow morning."

"That you will. We can continue our lively discussion then."

Kate turned away from her without speaking and inserted her card into the slot on the door. The tiny green light flashed, and she opened the door and stepped inside. Just inside the doorway, her sock-clad foot slid across something in a plastic bag on the floor. She skated forward like a bare tire on wet pavement and made a frantic but futile grab for the doorframe. As she crashed to the floor for the third time that night, she thought morosely that at least no one could accuse her of failing to add variety to her many misfortunes.

Shawn was stunned. One second, she was staring at the back of Kate Winston's head of short hair. The next second, she was staring at . . . nothing.

What the fuck?

She looked down. Kate was on the floor again. She'd gone down so quietly that Shawn wouldn't even have noticed if she'd turned away when Kate unlocked her door.

"What the hell happened?" she asked, squatting behind her.

"What the hell do you think happened?" Kate replied.

"You fell again?"

Kate let out a slow breath. "I bet you were the brightest one in your class, weren't you?"

Shawn ignored the remark. "Why did you fall? Is it your ankle?"

"No." Kate rummaged around on the floor and pulled something out from beneath her butt. "I slipped on this." She looked it over, and then held it up in disgust. "Welcome to CLIT-Con."

Shawn took it from her. It was a flimsy plastic bag filled with handouts and brochures advertising attractions in and around San Diego. There also were a couple dozen, brightly-colored pellet-like items loose in the bag.

"What are these little bead-like things?" she asked, holding the bag up to the light.

Kate craned her neck around to look, too. She grabbed the corner of the bag and rubbed a few of them together. "You've got to be kidding me."

"What?" Shawn looked at her.

"They're fucking Tic Tacs. Who the hell would put Tic Tacs loose in a bag on the floor?"

Shawn thought about it.

"Someone who's out drumming up business for a personal injury lawyer?"

"Why didn't they just use ball bearings? There certainly can't be any shortage of those at this damn conference."

"Now, now." Shawn wagged an index finger at her. "Take care not to indulge in any of those stereotypes you hate so much."

"Go to hell."

Shawn slowly shook her head. "Tell me. Does that thing hurt?"

"Does what thing hurt?"

"That stick up your ass. By my calculation, this is the third time tonight you've wound up sitting on it."

"I reiterate—go to hell."

Kate tried to shift herself into a different position so she could stand up. She winced in pain and dropped back to the floor.

"Let me help you stand up," Shawn offered.

Kate shook her head.

"Oh, come on," Shawn persisted. "I'll just help you inside and then I'll leave you alone to sit and brood in uninterrupted solitude."

Kate sat there another few seconds, then she sighed. "All right. But I'm only agreeing because I don't want to spend the night sitting here on this hideous carpet."

Shawn nodded. "It does sort of clash with your ensemble."

"You think? It looks like a damn reject from the Heywood Hale Broun collection."

Shawn reached beneath Kate's arms and lifted her up into a standing position. "You know, you're actually pretty funny—when you're not busy gnawing the entrails of fledgling authors."

Kate winced. Shawn wasn't sure if she was trying to suppress a smile, or because of the effort it took for her to stand up. It was clear that her ankle was hurting a lot.

"Put your arm around my neck," Shawn suggested. "It'll be easier for you to walk."

Kate looked dubious.

"I promise that I won't take advantage of your weakened state and cop a feel like your fans at the erotic table downstairs."

"You saw that?"

Shawn nodded. "It was kind of hard to miss. I mean, you don't get to see a nice ass coated with cheese every day."

"Oh god." Kate gingerly draped an arm around Shawn's shoulders. "I'll never live this down."

"Buck up, Brünnhilde. If this Dorothy Parker gig doesn't work out, you can always go back to being chief of the Valkyries."

"Anybody ever tell you that you're annoying and a total wiseass?"

Shawn laughed. "Add frumpy and you could be channeling my mother."

They started the slow journey across Kate's room.

"Your mother thinks you're a frumpy and annoying wiseass?"

Shawn nodded. "And an old maid."

"I think I like her."

"She's a Jew from Lower Merion who has elevated misery to the level of art."

"Now I know I like her."

"Either you're a freak with a fondness for scrapple and the Mummer's Day Parade, or you're just eager to side with anyone who wholly disapproves of me."

"Are these the only options?"

Shawn nodded.

"Yes."

"I should have left you in the hallway."

"But you didn't," Kate said. She winced again as they reached an overstuffed armchair. Shawn kicked its matching ottoman to the side so she could help her sit down.

"Why not?"

"Because you already said I had a nice ass."

"Don't let that go to your head, Blogula. I happen to think that anything covered in cheese is nice."

"A woman of discrimination."

"So unlike yourself."

"And by the way . . . Blogula?"

Shawn nodded enthusiastically. "Like it? It's kind of a pet name I have for you."

"Charming." Kate shook her head. "Well, I guess it's no worse than Eraserhead."

"You know about that one?"

Kate gave her a withering look.

"In fact," Shawn stood back and looked her over, "I think your haircut is quite utilitarian."

"Utilitarian?"

"Sure. It gives you a great place to store all those discarded cocktail picks."

Kate rolled her eyes. "Okay. You've earned your Girl Scout badge for this evening. Why don't you mosey along and find another place to exercise your beneficence?"

"Are you trying to get rid of me?"

"Now I'm certain that you were the brightest one in your class."

Shawn sighed. "Well, I guess I could go and get a head start on setting up my cookie concession."

"Off you go." Kate waved a hand. "Save me a box of Tagalongs."

"How about we score you a couple of Ibuprofen, instead?" Shawn pointed at her ankle. "It might help keep the swelling down."

Kate sighed. "You really are a glutton for punishment, aren't you?"

"Apparently. I even watched all twenty-seven of the Republican Primary debates."

"Ahh. You're a glutton and a masochist."

"Oh, come on. Don't tell me that you didn't manage to get caught up in any of the national Tea Party road show. It made for better TV than back-to-back episodes of Pawn Stars."

Kate looked confused. "There's a Presidential election this year?"

Shawn rolled her eyes. ""Nice try. How about that Ibuprofen? Got anything like that here?"

"As a matter of fact, I do, but I can't take any right now."

"Why not?"

"Well, it's Advil P.M., and I haven't eaten anything since this morning. I think it would knock me on my ass."

Shawn tried not to smile. As soon as the words were out of Kate's mouth, she realized what she had said. She dropped her head into her hands.

"Somebody up there hates me."

Shawn patted the toe of the one shoe Kate still had on. "No worries, Eraserhead. Help is still at hand."

She went to the telephone on top of a nightstand and picked up the receiver.

Kate lifted her head. "What do you think you're doing?"

"Ordering you some dinner."

"You can't do that."

"Sure I can." Shawn ran a fingertip down the directory of services printed on the face of the telephone. "How to call room service was the first thing they taught us in Scouting. Well, right after we learned how to make a travois out of drapery rods and discarded bikini wax strips. See?" She punched in a sequence of numbers. "You just push these little buttons, and presto. Minions way down in the bowels of the hotel rush to minister to your every need."

"Where the hell was this Girl Scout troop?"

Shawn held the receiver up to her ear. "I told you . . . Main Line Philadelphia."

"It figures."

"Hello? Room Service? Yes. This is Miss Winston in Room 816. I'd like to order a . . ." She looked at Kate with a raised eyebrow.

Kate sighed. "A cobb salad."

"A cobb salad," Shawn repeated.

"But no hardboiled egg."

"No hardboiled egg," Shawn said.

"And no croutons, but extra bacon."

Shawn dropped the phone to her chest and stared at Kate.

Kate shrugged.

Shawn tried again. "No croutons, but add extra bacon."

Kate wasn't finished. "No processed cheese, either."

Shawn sighed and closed her eyes. "No cheese."

"I didn't say *no* cheese," Kate hissed. "I said no *processed* cheese."

Shawn counted to three. "Can you tell me what kinds of cheese you have?" She listened, and then turned to Kate.

"They have cheddar, Swiss, parmesan, Monterey Jack, and bleu."

Kate thought about it. "Is the bleu cheese made from soy?"

Shawn barely refrained from strangling Kate. "Fuck the cheese. What kind of dressing?"

"Vinaigrette," Kate said.

"Vinaigrette dressing," Shawn said into the phone.

"But only if it's made with EVOO," Kate added. "And I want it on the side."

Shawn had had enough. "Listen," she said to the minion on the line. "Forget all of that bullshit and just bring me a bacon double cheeseburger with an extra-large side of fries."

Kate looked horrified. "Are you crazy?"

Shawn ignored her. "That's right. And make it two of each."

"I am so not eating that."

Shawn looked at her. "You'll eat it all right, and you'll pay for it, too."

Kate thought about it. "Extra mustard."

Shawn smiled. "Extra mustard. And throw in a bottle of Darioush and two glasses."

.

"I don't agree with that at all."

Kate was sopping up the last of the mustard with a soggy French fry.

"Of course you don't," Shawn said. "If you ever agreed with me about anything, you'd have to enter a witness relocation program."

"That's not true," Kate said. She held up her wine glass. "What about this?"

"I don't think this counts."

"Why not?"

"Oh come on. Who wouldn't like a really fine Shiraz?"

"You saw the Gyno Galaxy series, right?"

Shawn sighed. "You know I did."

"Oh, that's right. You did go down on it . . . in a manner of speaking."

"Very funny."

"Your gymnastic feats aside, V. Jay-Jay Singh has been known to open beer bottles with her . . . well . . ."

Shawn was intrigued. "With her what?"

"Use your imagination."

Shawn thought about that for few moments. "No way!"

"Way."

"Nuh uh."

"Uh huh."

"I don't believe you."

"I don't really care."

Shawn looked down in the general vicinity of her own . . . opener and shuddered. "That's not even possible."

Kate shrugged.

"Is it?"

Kate shrugged again.

"And they think we'd be a better draw for the opening session than that?"

"Shawn, I really don't think they thought about having V. Jay-Jay demonstrate this particular gift."

"Too bad." Shawn sighed. "I think it would've attracted truckers from ten states."

"Trust me. Anything named CLIT-Con would attract truckers."

"Yeah, but they'd all think it was something that required penicillin."

"They certainly could've sold a shitload of koozies."

Shawn snagged another French fry from Kate's plate. "Did you eat all the mustard?"

"Beggars can't be choosers."

"What's that supposed to mean?"

"Well, you did eat all of your fries and half of mine."

"Yeah? Well you ate all of your burger and half of mine."

"Did not."

"Did, too."

"I only ate your bacon. It's not the same thing."

"It is when it's sitting on top of a bacon cheeseburger."

Kate sighed. "Eating the bacon hardly qualifies as eating half of the sandwich."

"Does, too."

"Does not."

"Does, too!"

"See?" Kate rolled her eyes. "This is exactly what I meant when I pointed out your fondness for excessive statement."

"Gimme a break, Winston. One thing has nothing to do with the other."

Shawn shifted her weight. They were sitting side by side on Kate's big bed with all the food spread out across the space between them. Kate's sore ankle was propped up on a stack of extra pillows. Shawn hadn't intended to stay in Kate's room to eat, but when the food arrived, Kate told her it was ridiculous to schlep it halfway across the hotel again, and that she should stay and eat her portion while it was still semi-hot.

Shawn could never say no to any woman who correctly used the word schlep.

Or to any woman who put mustard on her French fries.

They'd been trying to find safe topics to discuss, and had drifted into a conversation about trends in lesbian fiction. Shawn was surprised to discover that Kate actually had a balanced and informed perspective about most aspects of the genre. Plus she seemed to be on a first-name basis with all of the leading authors and publishers. It soon became clear that, although there were many things she liked about the literature—if you could call it that—she abided in frustration that so much of it was cloying and repetitive. And that shortcoming, in her view, could be laid squarely at the feet of the publishers, who did little to push, cajole, or insist that their authors move beyond the safety nets of the familiar.

And where the hell were the editors?

Kate told Shawn that she once, in disgust, took the time to count all of the adverbs used in a book she had been asked to review.

"When I got up to eight hundred and fifty, I quit counting, and I wasn't even halfway through the damn thing."

Shawn was amazed. "Seriously. How could an editor brazenly allow such appallingly deficient prose to see the enthusiastically blinding light of a gloriously new day?"

Kate scowled at her. "Fuck you and the reflexive pronoun you rode in on."

"Did you just end a sentence with a preposition?"

"Oh, my bad," Kate said without a trace of contrition. "Fuck you and the reflexive pronoun you rode in on, bitch."

Shawn slowly shook her head. "Are you always this crusty?"

"I don't know," Kate replied. "Are you always this annoying?"

"You'd have to ask my marketing guru that question."

Kate nodded. "I think I begin to understand why she spent most of the evening in the beverage line, two-fisting tall boys."

"Oh really," Shawn asked with interest. "Was V. Jay-Jay opening them for her? I always did suspect that Gwen's tastes ran to the exotic."

Kate actually smiled. "That could lend new meaning to your title."

"*Bottle Rocket?*"

Kate nodded.

Shawn laughed out loud. "Now there's an idea for some cover art that would rival the best of what's on display downstairs."

"Oh, god." Kate raised her eyes to the ceiling. "Don't even get me started on that part of this business. Most of those books look like . . . I don't know." She waved a hand. "What's the same sex term for bodice ripper?"

Shawn thought about it. "Carhartt cutter?"

Kate laughed. "Flannel flayer?"

"Boot buster."

"Chap chafer."

"Saddle soaper."

"Jersey jerker."

Shawn raised an eyebrow. "Jersey jerker?"

Kate shrugged. "I was channeling women's basketball."

"Oh. Okay. That works."

Kate drained her wine glass. "I don't suppose there's any more of this, is there?"

Shawn grabbed the bottle off the end table next to her side of the bed. She held it up sideways. "I'm sad to report that Elvis has left the building."

"No he hasn't." Kate giggled. "I saw him getting off the elevator about three hours ago."

"For real?"

Kate nodded. "He was all wrapped around Vivien K. O'Reilly. I think he's moderating a session tomorrow."

"Ours?"

"In your dreams, Sparky."

Shawn sighed. "Too bad."

"Why?"

"I thought it might provide some much needed comic relief."

Kate snorted. "Oh really? How? By having him belt out a few rousing choruses of 'Don't Be Cruel' to warm up the room?"

"It could work." Shawn bumped Kate's shoulder. "Besides, isn't that your signature tune?"

"I don't have a signature tune."

"Of course you do. Everybody does."

Kate seemed intrigued. "Oh really?"

Shawn nodded.

"Okay, wiseass. What's yours?"

Shawn smiled. "Clearly, you don't understand how signature tunes work. I don't get to pick one. It evolves . . . organically."

"Organically?"

Shawn nodded again.

Kate looked dubious. "I haven't known you very long, but there seems to be precious little about you that could ever be called organic."

"Pish posh."

"Pish posh?"

Shawn shrugged.

"You're such a nerd. If you did have a signature tune, it would have to be something retro and annoying."

"Like?"

"I don't know." Kate chewed the inside of her cheek. "Maybe something by The Archies."

Shawn sat up straighter. "I loved The Archies."

"You would."

"Hey. You can't hold having unrefined musical tastes against me. The soundtrack of my formative years was comprised mostly of polkas."

"And Barbra Streisand."

Shawn didn't deny it. "It was pretty pathetic. In retrospect, I wonder if my mother's cherished subscription to the Columbia Record Club was part of their 'Turn Your Child Into a Serial Killer' package."

"It could be. Ever enjoy torturing small animals?"

Shawn sighed. "Nope. Just bloggers."

"That figures."

"I know. Lucky you."

Kate eyed her. "Opinions on that differ."

They fell quiet. Shawn could hear the sound of muffled laughter coming from the hallway outside Kate's room. Things seemed to be heating up. It was no secret that most of the real action at CLIT-Con took place after hours on the floors above the conference venue.

She glanced at her watch. It was nearly midnight. Kate wasn't looking at her. The quiet between them seemed unnatural.

Shawn suddenly felt uncomfortable as hell, and she didn't really know why.

She decided that flight was her best option.

"I really need to go," she said. "It's awfully late, and I should never have stayed this long."

Kate didn't reply.

Shawn collected their empty plates and stacked them on the service tray. "Thanks for the meal."

"No problem," Kate replied. She wasn't looking at Shawn. She was too busy smoothing out a crease on the bedspread. "Thanks for helping me back to the room."

Shawn stood up, carried the tray to a small desk, and set it down, then thought better of it. "Do you want me to put this outside the door?"

Kate shook her head. "I'll deal with it later."

Shawn continued to stand in front of her, feeling like she needed to say something else, but not knowing quite what. "Will you be okay?" It was lame, but it was the best she could come up with.

Kate raised her eyes and looked at her. There was only one lamp turned on the room, but Shawn could still see how blue her eyes were.

"I'll be fine." She patted the knee of her affected leg. "It feels a lot better already."

"Okay." Shawn picked up her gym towel and room key. "I guess I'll see you tomorrow morning."

"That you will."

The short walk to the door felt like Lee's retreat from the battle at Gettysburg. She was sure that Kate was watching her, and that made her feel clumsy and inelegant. What the hell had happened to the almost easy camaraderie they seemed to be inching toward? Shawn was actually starting to relax about the session tomorrow. Correction— today. But something changed when they heard the laughter outside the door, and they both retreated to their corners like boxers after the clang of a bell.

The door loomed in front of her like the entrance to a tomb.

That wasn't right. It was more like an exit than an entrance. And she knew that once she was on the other side of it, calm and reason would be restored. Right now, she felt like a pinball machine on tilt. She grabbed the door handle, and the big dead bolt lock unlatched with a loud click. She stepped halfway out of the room and looked down the hall.

Her blood ran cold.

No fucking way.

She took a half step back and hovered in the doorway so she could take a second look.

God. It was even more horrifying a second time.

She backed into the room as quickly as she could and slammed the door shut.

"What the hell is going on?" Kate's voice rang out from her prone position on the bed.

Shawn stood with her back against the door, taking deep breaths. "I can't talk about it."

"Oh, good god." Kate climbed down off the bed and limped to the door. "What's the matter with you?"

Shawn held her gym towel up to her eyes. "I think I'm blind."

Kate shoved her away from the door and reached for the handle. "Move over."

"You can't go out there." Shawn barred her way.

"Why the fuck not?"

"Because I saw Gwen," Shawn hissed. "And it was terrifying."

"You saw Gwen?"

Shawn nodded.

Kate held out her hands. "That's what has you in such a swivet?"

Shawn nodded again.

"What am I missing here?"

"She was . . ." Shawn made an oblique gesture.

"She was what?"

Shawn held up her hand. "Just trust me on this. You don't want to know."

Kate grabbed Shawn by the arm and hauled her away from the door. "I'll make my own assessment, thank you." She craned her neck and looked through the peephole. After a moment, she turned to Shawn with an expression of exasperation. "You're crazy. There's nothing out there but a hundred miles of bad carpet."

"Just wait a minute," Shawn replied. "She'll be back."

"Back? Back from where?"

"The ice machine. She was carrying a big bucket full of long necks."

"Long necks?"

Shawn nodded.

"Really?"

Shawn nodded again.

"Could you tell what kind?" Kate sounded intrigued now.

"I'm not positive, but it looked like PBR."

"PBR?" Enlightenment spread across Kate's features. "Interesting. This is definitely gonna be worth watching." She turned back to the peephole. After another minute, she fluttered a hand back and forth in excitement. "Here she comes," she whispered. "Oh. My. God."

Shawn tried to push her aside. "Let me see."

"Quit shoving me," Kate hissed. "You've already seen her."

"Come on. I saw her first." Shawn elbowed her way in so that they both were vying for space in front of the tiny peephole.

"Oh god," Shawn said. "Is she wearing what I think she's wearing?"

Kate's face was millimeters away from hers. Even in her excitement, Shawn didn't miss that her hair smelled great—like ginger and oranges.

"Yep," Kate said. "That's Quinn's, all right."

Gwen was walking past Kate's room, carrying a bucket that was overloaded with beer bottles and ice. Tiny cubes of ice were falling out as she walked along, disappearing into the rust and brown abyss of the carpet. She was wearing an oversized black t-shirt—and nothing else. No pants, no shoes, no nothing. When she passed the door, they could clearly read the message emblazoned across the back of her shirt.

"I guess the bitch fell off," Shawn whispered.

"Jesus Christ," Kate muttered. "Is that a dog collar? And what are those bracelet-looking things on her ankles?"

Shawn nudged her. "Excuse me . . . but aren't you the same woman who reviewed the immortal classic, MILF Money?"

"Fuck you."

"You know," Shawn said. "Normally, I'd just refer a detractor like you to my marketing guru, but now I'd worry about your safety."

"Is that supposed to make me feel better?" Kate asked, turning to her. Their noses were nearly touching.

"Um. Yes?" Shawn wasn't thinking very clearly right then. Kate's eyes glowed like Ohio Blue Tips—the kind her grandmother used to use to light the gas burners on her kitchen stove.

"These conferences are notorious for hookups like this," Kate said. She was still speaking in a whisper, although by now, Gwen was far beyond earshot.

"So I've heard." Shawn had never noticed how beautiful Kate's mouth was—when it wasn't spewing vitriol.

"I think behavior like this is contemptible." She was speaking so low that Shawn was having a hard time hearing her.

"What?" Shawn moved in a little closer. Kate grabbed hold of her arms to avoid falling on her gimpy ankle.

"I said," Kate whispered. "This kind of behavior is . . ."

"Is what?"

"Contemptible," Kate said. "It's contemptible."

Shawn could feel little wisps of air against her face when Kate spoke. It wasn't at all unpleasant. "I agree. They should exercise more self-control."

Kate nodded. The scent from her hair was driving Shawn crazy. It smelled like summer. She wanted to bury her face in it.

"I don't know why I keep coming to these," Kate said. "It's the same thing every year."

"Maybe you think you'll get lucky, too?"

Kate raised her eyes to Shawn's. "Do you think I need to get lucky?"

There was something vaguely coquettish in the way she asked the question. Shawn now felt like she was the one who was unsteady on her feet.

"No," she said, tugging Kate closer. "That's not what I think."

Kate didn't try to pull away. "What do you think?"

"I think I'm about to violate about twenty-five conflict of interest clauses." She inched her head forward and lightly kissed, then licked at Kate's lips. She heard a low-pitched moan, and realized it was coming from one of them. Or maybe it was coming from both of them. It was hard to tell.

Kate was breathing heavily now. "You know," she ran a hand up Shawn's arm and along behind her neck, "there was one thing I was curious about when I finished reading your book."

"And that was?"

Kate tugged her head down and gave her an incendiary kiss. It went on and on. When they finally came up for air, they were leaning heavily against the door. Shawn's legs felt like rubber, and she was pretty sure Kate's did, too.

"I wondered," Kate whispered as she bit Shawn's earlobe, "what you could possibly come up with as an encore."

As soon as Shawn commenced showing her, Kate's legs gave out, and she dropped to the floor for the fourth time that night. Only, this time, there was a soft and willing debut author on hand to break her fall.

"Where the hell have you been?"

Gwen was pissed, and she wasn't doing much to conceal it.

The opening session was due to start in less than twenty minutes, and Shawn had only just shown up. She was carrying an extra-large cup of coffee and a bagel, and had a dog-eared copy of Bottle Rocket tucked beneath her arm. She hadn't eaten any breakfast, so she stopped off at the concession area set up at the back of the Indigo Level Ballroom to scare up something to eat.

She hadn't had time to do much of anything that morning except grab a speed shower and change her clothes. Fortunately for her, the down elevator was more cooperative, and did not stop on every floor.

"I didn't get much sleep last night," Shawn apologized. And neither did you, she was tempted to add.

In fact, Gwen didn't look any the worse for wear, which was surprising, considering the night she'd probably had. Shawn could see some slight discoloration on the parts of her neck that were visible beneath the scarf she wore.

Ewww. Best not to think about that.

"I called your room and texted you about fifty times," Gwen continued.

Shawn took a bite out of her bagel. "Why? Did the bar run out of vegan wine?"

"Very funny." Gwen grabbed her by the elbow and pulled her to stand behind a massive potted palm, causing the several shy types who had been lurking there to scurry away like cockroaches fleeing the glare of an overhead light. The hall was really filling up. There were at least two hundred people milling around, and as many already seated.

"You won't believe who called me this morning." Gwen's mood transitioned from pissed to excited. "Go ahead. Guess."

"The CDC?" Shawn asked.

"No." Gwen narrowed her eyes. "Why the hell would I get a call from the Center for Disease Control?"

Shawn shrugged. "Blame the CSI marathon I watched all night."

"Whatever." Gwen waved a dismissive hand, then she appeared to catch sight of something over Shawn's shoulder. Her agitation returned, and she manically straightened her scarf. "Don't look now, but someone very special just entered the hall," she said in a low voice.

Shawn rolled her eyes. "Who? Barbara Walters?" She took a big sip of her coffee.

Gwen's eyes grew round. "How'd you know? Damn that blabbermouth Barb Davis. I told her not to tell you."

Shawn choked and spewed coffee all over the palm. Gwen barely had time to skip out of the way. Shawn's coughing jag went on and on, and her eyes filled up with tears. Gwen took the steaming cup out of her hand and patted her on the back until she dislodged a partially chewed hunk of bagel.

Shawn wiped at her eyes. "You've got to be kidding me." Her voice was husky.

"Nope. That's why I kept trying to find you. Her people contacted me last night. They've been following your online feud with Kate Winston, and they want to include you two in an upcoming special she's doing on gay culture for ABC news."

"You've got to be kidding me."

"No, I'm not kidding you. Yes, it's happening, and with Ba-Ba herself. She happened to be in San Diego this week, so she decided to come by this morning to catch the fireworks." She lowered her voice. "I'm counting on you to make sure she's not disappointed. If this goes well, not only will you be on your way to a mainstream publishing career, Kate Winston could very well end up with a recurring slot on *Good Morning America*."

"You've got to be kidding me."

Gwen sighed. "Do I need to slap you?"

Shawn shook her head. "I think I'm having an out-of-body experience."

"Trust me. Anyone who can cough up a wad of masticated bread and shoot it halfway across a room the size of an airplane hangar, definitely is not having an out-of-body experience."

Shawn groaned. Why was this happening now? A thought occurred to her. She looked at Gwen, who was busy scanning the room, probably trying to pinpoint Ba-Ba's location.

"Does Kate Winston know about this yet?"

Gwen met her eyes. "I'd assume so. Linda Evans was going to give her the happy news."

Happy news?

107

If it was such happy news, then why did Shawn suddenly feel so miserable? She didn't want to spar with Kate. Not any more, and certainly not on national T.V. Not after last night. Last night had been amazing. Last night had been incredible. Last night had been full of mystery and innovation—a no-holds-barred practicum on lesbian romance. Last night had been like a tour of the romance writer's ultimate laboratory—a giant petri dish, brimming with hackneyed clichés and overblown conventions that were growing like wild flowers.

Last night had laid waste to all of her sanctimonious protestations that mind-blowing sex never happened on a first encounter.

And last night had also been a testament to how many stains a two-ounce packet of mustard could make on a set of hotel sheets.

"What's the matter with you?" Gwen asked. "I thought you'd be in transports about this. It's the break we've been waiting for."

Transports? Shawn thought. I'd like to be on a goddamn transport. Out of here, and away from this whole mess.

"I just need a little time to adjust to the news," she said instead. "And I'm a little nervous about this session."

Gwen handed the cup of coffee back to her. "You'll do just fine. If you feel yourself tensing up, just remember everything the bitch said."

She remembered, all right. The things Kate said to her last night would cause her toes to curl up inside her shoes.

In fact, her toes were curling up right now.

Gwen straightened. "There she is. I gotta go make nice. You get ready to knock her socks off." She patted Shawn on the arm. "Make us proud." She walked off so quickly that leaves on the palm rustled in her wake.

Shawn stood there in a daze.

Oy, gevalt.

"Say that again?"

Kate was certain she'd misunderstood Linda.

Her editor had caught up with her just as she was about to limp into one of the hotel's four thousand Starbucks cafés. The damn things were omnipresent—about as plentiful as the massive potted palms that seemed to be the hallmark of this joint.

"I said Barbara Walters is here to catch the opening session, and

ABC News is sniffing around you as a possible weekend contributor to *GMA*."

Kate was stunned. "*GMA?*"

Linda nodded. "How about that? This feud between you and Shawn Harris has been the best thing to happen to lesbian fiction since Radclyffe Hall got her first haircut. It's a gold mine, Kate, and it's going to launch both of you into the national spotlight. And the notice you're bringing to the entire genre will open doors for lots of others, too."

"I need coffee."

"You need coffee?" Linda was incredulous. "This is your reaction? You need coffee?"

Kate looked at her in a daze. "If you want something more dramatic, I could probably throw up on your shoes."

Linda took her by the arm and hauled her inside the small lobby café. It took her a moment to notice that Kate was walking unsteadily. "What's wrong with your leg?"

"It's not my leg, it's my ankle. I twisted it last night in the gym." Kate held up a hand to forestall Linda's further expressions of concern. "It's not that bad, I promise."

"Well, shit. Let's find you a place to sit down. I'll get us some coffee."

Kate nodded.

"Try to relax." Linda glanced at her watch. "We've got about twenty-five minutes before show time."

Kate plopped down on the first unoccupied sofa she came to. She didn't even bother to brush the ubiquitous trail of crumbs off its stiff cushions.

Oh god. This was not happening. Not now. Not this way.

"Do you want something to eat?" Linda asked. "You do look pretty green around the gills."

Kate looked up at her. "What?" She had no idea what Linda had just said.

"Food," Linda repeated. "Do you want something to eat?"

Kate shook her head. "No. Thanks. Just coffee."

Linda nodded and walked off toward the counter. Kate watched her go.

"Extra hot," she called out.

Linda stopped and turned around. "Is that it?"

"Venti."

"Okaaayyy." Linda turned back toward the waiting barista.

"With an extra shot."

"Right." Linda called over her shoulder.

"No cream."

Linda stopped and faced her.

"Seriously?"

Kate shrugged.

"Anything else?"

Kate thought about it. "Maybe a biscotti?"

Linda sighed. "Okay."

"But not one of the chocolate ones."

"Kate," Linda said with more than a trace of annoyance, "is your goal to get me to throw up on my own shoes? If so, you're doing great."

"Sorry," Kate apologized. "I'm a little off my game this morning."

"Well, try to calm down. We need to focus." She glanced at her watch again. "Now let me get us some coffee before we run out of time."

Kate nodded, and Linda walked off.

Oh my god, she thought. Why is this happening now?

The night with Shawn had been amazing. Surreal. It changed the entire landscape of her life in ways she never would have believed possible. By mutual consent, they had agreed to bury the hatchet—publicly. But now? Now what?

And what did Shawn know about this? Anything? They had only parted about an hour ago, and neither of them had bothered to check their messages. They'd been too . . . preoccupied to care.

And she had a headache, to boot. It was from that damn second bottle of wine they drank. Something horrible that had been in the CLIT-Con welcome basket. Who in the hell thought it was a good idea to buy wine from a vineyard in Indiana?

Her head was spinning. She needed to talk with Shawn. She looked over her shoulder at the counter. Linda was still standing there, bent over the glass cabinet, pointing to some kind of confection.

She pulled out her cell phone and typed a quick message.

Kate Winston
Where are you?

Ten seconds later, her phone buzzed.

Shawn Harris
I'm in the ballroom. I've been looking all over for you.

Kate Winston
We HAVE to talk.

Shawn Harris
No shit, Sherlock! Have you heard the news?

Kate Winston
Yes! I'm with Linda right now.

Shawn Harris
What the hell are we going to do?

Kate Winston
The only thing we CAN do. We're going to have to go
through with it.

Shawn Harris
Oh shit. What if I came down with something?

Kate Winston
Like what???

Shawn Harris
I don't know . . . how about Legionnaire's Disease?

Kate Winston
Shawn . . .

Shawn Harris
Hey . . . I'm doing the best I can on short notice.

Kate Winston
Right.

Shawn Harris
I mean it!

Kate Winston
Face it, Sparky . . . we're going to have to go through
with it.

Shawn Harris
How? It's fucking Barbara Walters.

Kate Winston
I know.

Shawn Harris
Okay, genius. What's your plan?

Kate Winston
I don't HAVE a plan. We're just going to have to give them
what they want.

Shawn Harris
You mean continue to pretend that we hate each other?

Kate Winston
Yes. According to Linda, the success of the entire lesbian
publishing world now hinges on the media circus generated
by our feud.

Shawn Harris
Give me a break!

Kate Winston
I think that's precisely what this is, Sparky: a BIG break—for
each of us.

Shawn Harris
Are you sure?

Kate thought about that. Was she sure? It was what they both wanted. They'd talked about it last night, while they drank that nasty Indiana wine. Shawn said that her ultimate fantasy—besides the one or two more esoteric ones they'd already satisfied—was to write a crossover novel that would have equal appeal to a mainstream audience. Kate confessed that her goal was to become a regular columnist for one of the leading media syndicates.

She looked up. Linda was on her way back with a tray containing two cups of coffee and some kind of enormous sugarcoated something.

Kate Winston
Yes. I'm sure. Look . . . Linda is coming. I gotta go.

Shawn Harris
Okay. I guess we'll find out. Hey, Poodle?

Kate Winston
Yes, Sparky?

Shawn Harris
I had a great time last night.

Kate smiled. She felt like a schoolgirl who'd just been passed a note on the bus.

Kate Winston
Me, too.

Now it just remained to see what they could make of it.

She tucked her phone back into her shoulder bag and waited on Linda.

Barbara Walters. Good god.

Cricket MacBean, the moderator of the Con's opening session, was a tough, no-nonsense ex-Army nurse who took no prisoners. That's why Barb Davis chose her for this impossible assignment. Cricket was the editor of a prestigious series of lesbian fiction anthologies. She knew everybody and took shit from nobody. Barb described her as an unrepentant M*A*S*H nurse on steroids, and that made her the perfect candidate to manage a session that was sure to become a raucous, free-for-all.

The hall was packed. Late last night, Con organizers had begged, pleaded, and cajoled their way into one of the hotel's largest ballrooms after Barb found out that three busses loaded with Sapphic book clubbers were en route to San Diego from Portland—the lesbian mecca of the great northwest. Fortunately, hotel personnel were able to move the "Honoring Your Marriage Vows In Accordance With Biblical Principles" group into a smaller venue down the hall. More than one Hilton employee expressed concern about the wisdom of the last minute change and worried that no amount of signage would be sufficient to keep the two groups separated.

It was anybody's guess. In any case, it was Cricket's problem now.

At the crack of ten, she banged her gavel, and the Plenary Session of the Fourteenth Annual Creative Literary Insights and Trends Conference was underway. After some opening announcements the two antagonists were introduced, and the hall erupted into a cacophony of applause, cat calls, wolf whistles, and boos.

Kate and Shawn were seated on opposite sides of a riser located at the front of the giant meeting space. Cricket stood between them. The feisty redhead barely topped the tall podium, but made up for it in attitude as she laid out the rules of engagement.

"Go ahead and get this noise out of your systems," she shouted over the din. "Because once we get started, there won't be any more of these outbursts. If you don't think you can conduct yourselves appropriately, I invite you to collect your crullers and leave." She stood, stone-faced, until the whooping and hollering quieted to a titter.

Cricket glared at the crowd over the rims of her half-eye glasses.

"Welcome to our opening session, 'The Good, the Bad, and the Ugly: Dealing with Negative Reviews.' Our two special guests are Shawn Harris, author of the bestselling novel *Bottle Rocket*, and Kate Winston, blogger and book critic for the online journal, *Gilded Lily*. After brief opening remarks, we'll get the ball rolling with a few pre-pared questions. Then we'll open it up to the audience. There are two microphones up here on stands at opposite sides of the stage. If I call on you, please come forward to ask your question. There will be only one question at a time—no exceptions. Is everyone clear about how this will work?"

There were nods all around the room.

"Good." Cricket turned to Shawn. "Shawn, if you would be so kind? Step forward and start us off."

Shawn stood up and approached the center of the stage to a thunderous round of applause. Cricket allowed it to continue for about twenty seconds, then shut it down by slamming her gavel repeatedly on the podium.

Shawn stepped up to take Cricket's place behind the mike and looked out over the sea of faces.

"Thanks, Cricket," she said. "And thank you to the organizers of this conference for giving me the opportunity to be here with all of you today. Thanks, too, to our colleague, Kate Winston, for agreeing to participate in this important discussion." She placed her notecards down on the slanted top of the podium. "*Bottle Rocket* is a novel about the futility and emptiness of a life without aspirations, and the salvation that is borne of strength and hope."

With those words, the San Diego CLIT-Con commenced its fabled journey toward myth, legend, and forty-two cases of aggravated assault.

Things were heating up.

The questions were getting more and more fractious, and Cricket was banging her gavel with more energy and frequency. Kate was certain she'd heard the sound of wood splintering during that last round of frenzied hammering.

A frizzy-haired zealot wearing snakeskin jackboots was at the mike right now, demanding to know why Gilded Lily hadn't fired Kate's ass for maligning the integrity of one of the "best writers in all of lesfic."

In fact, Kate would have been hard-pressed to explain that one herself.

As discreetly as she could, she sent Shawn a text message. They'd been communicating this way pretty much since the start of the session.

Kate Winston
What is it with your fans and the funky-ass footwear?

Shawn Harris
Python is very hot this year.

Kate Winston
How the hell am I supposed to respond to this question?

Shawn Harris
Hand her off to Linda. All she's doing is sitting there in the front row, pretending not to stare at Barbara Walters.

Kate Winston
GREAT idea! Sparky?

Shawn Harris
Yes, Poodle?

Kate Winston
You know what else is hot this year?

Shawn Harris
Enlighten me.

Kate Winston
You are.

Shawn Harris
Oh, gosh. Eraserhead? You say the sweeeeeetest things.

Bang! Bang! Bang! Bang!
Kate jumped and nearly dropped her cell phone.
Cricket was smacking the podium so hard that shards of wood were flying up around her head like sparks from an acetylene torch. The noise in the hall was getting out of control again. Members of the pro-Kate faction were trying to drown out Ms. Python Boots by banging empty Frappucino bottles against their tabletops, causing the pro-Shawn types to retaliate by pelting the drummers with some of the cellophane-wrapped Starlight mints that sat in bowls on each table.
CLIT-Con was famous for cheap candy.

"This behavior is unacceptable!" Cricket yelled into the microphone. "Take your seats right now, or we'll clear the room!"

A red- and white-striped mint whizzed by her ear.

"I saw that, Vivien." Cricket was fuming. "There will be no more of these sophomoric shenanigans, or partisan grandstanding. Do you understand me? Do not request to ask a question or make a comment unless you can behave with dignity and professionalism." She cast her eyes over the assembly, and the scores of raised hands. "You . . . standing there against the back wall? Do you have something appropriate to share?"

A well-dressed woman, wearing stilettos and black-patterned hose, nodded and slowly made her way to the front of the room. A chorus of catcalls followed her.

Kate Winston
Who in the hell is THAT?

Shawn Harris
Beats me. Maybe there's a breakout session on how to
improve your drag.

The questioner reached the microphone and held up a thick, leather-bound book.

"I didn't realize at first that I had stumbled into the wrong meeting room," she explained. "Although I did wonder why there were so many men with bad haircuts in here. Then I realized that I wasn't at the right meeting at all, and that this room was filled with perverted Naomis."

A cascade of boos grew up around her. She just talked louder.

"The Lord sent me here today for a reason—to tell you all that Leviticus 18:22 says ye shall not lie with a man as with a woman."

"You got that right, sister," someone yelled from the side of the room.

"Order!" Cricket slammed her gavel.

"Not unless he buys my ass dinner first."

"I said, come to order," Cricket repeated.

"Don't knock it until you've tried it, honey."

"That's enough." Cricket walked around to the front of her podium. "The next person who speaks out of turn will be forcibly evicted from this hall."

She gestured wildly at two hotel security guards who were stationed near the rear exit.

"Fuck that shit. It's a free country."

Cricket strode to the edge of the stage and pointed her gavel at a very large woman wearing ripped jeans and a white t-shirt with a bright purple labrys on it.

"My session. My rules."

"Kiss my ass."

"I'd love to, Cinderella," Cricket replied. "But in your case, that would be an all day job, and we only have the room until eleven-thirty."

The big bull dyke boiled over. "Fuck you, Loretta Swit!"

She grabbed a bagel loaded with cream cheese off the plate in front of her and let it fly in a fast-pitch throw that would've put Dot Richardson to shame. The white-topped disc sailed across the room with pinpoint accuracy and nailed Cricket squarely between the eyes. There was a collective gasp in the hall as the thing hung there, briefly frozen in time, before it slid down Cricket's face.

Cricket caught the bagel in her hand when it dropped from her chin.

She licked some of the cream cheese off her lips. "Chives," she said, hefting the half-eaten thing up and down. "Everybody knows that I. Hate. Chives."

Cricket exploded off the stage like a heat-seeking red projectile and crashed through half-a-dozen rows of attendees to reach her target.

"Incoming!" she roared as she slammed, full-throttle, into her assailant. "This'll shut you up, bitch!" She smashed the bagel into the woman's face and smeared the cream cheese all over her.

"Fight!" someone screamed.

"Get this crazy cunt off me," the woman beneath Cricket hollered.

Two bystanders tried without success to pull Cricket away.

"I will not be insulted," she screamed.

"They're attacking the moderator," someone yelled. "Let's get 'em, girls."

The two-dozen women who had been upended in Cricket's charge slapped and shoved at one another as they tried to untangle themselves from the heap of arms and legs they ended up in.

"Get your damn chair off my foot."

"Get your damn foot out of my crotch."

"Get your damn crotch out of my face."

"Get your damn hands off my boobs."

"Oh, my bad."

"Jesus, Viv . . ."

"Sorry."

The Honoring-Your-Marriage-Vows-In–Accordance-With-Biblical-Principles zealot still had possession of the microphone.

"Infidels," she droned on. "Lilith's. Jezebels. Turn from your sick and unnatural paths."

"Somebody cut her goddamn mike!" Barb Davis had fought her way to the front of the room. "And for god's sake, get Barbara Walters out of here." She looked around. "Where are those fucking security guards?"

She cast about for Shawn and Kate, but they were nowhere to be seen. "God fucking damn it. Now we've lost our headliners, too."

She saw Quinn Glatfelter standing next to one of the accordion walls used to divide the space into smaller venues. She was wrangling five women at the same time. They were hissing and spitting like Copperheads. It was hard to tell whether or not this activity was related to the riot—with Quinn, you never really knew for sure.

"Quinn," she yelled over the din. "Quinn!"

Quinn heard her and looked her way.

"Drop the bimbos and come get Barbara Walters out of here."

Quinn looked confused.

Barb pointed furiously toward the riser where Barbara Walters and her cameraman huddled with Linda Evans and Gwen Carlisle. They all seemed to be arguing about something. Gwen kept grabbing the arm of Barbara's cameraman, trying to get him to film something at the back of the room, and Linda was shaking her head in obvious disagreement. Barbara Walters just looked . . . like Barbara Walters. Poised, fascinated, and in complete control.

The cameraman just kept rolling. The red light on top of his Sony swung back and forth across the room like a neon metronome.

All Barb cared about was getting the celebrity news anchor and talk show host out of there before she got clocked by a flying chair. She'd signed a damage waiver when they rented the hotel space, and this effing brawl was going to bankrupt CLIT-Con's coffers for years to come—probably forever. She couldn't risk a personal injury lawsuit on top of it.

Quinn finally understood what Barb was asking her to do.

When she recognized the famous T.V. personality, she nodded and gave Barb a big, toothy smile. With a flick of both wrists, she sent all five of her hostages sprawling. In seconds, she'd plowed her way across the room and stopped at the foot of the riser where Linda and Gwen were vying to direct the cameraman. She saw Quinn say something to Barbara Walters, who just looked intrigued. Then Quinn grabbed Walters by the waist and tossed her over her massive shoulder in a ludicrous parody of a fireman's carry.

Barb just closed her eyes and looked away. There was no way this could get any worse.

Six anemic-looking hotel security guards with bad acne and baggy polyester pants were finally picking their way down what was left of the center aisle toward Barb.

Wrong, she thought. It just got worse.

"We're gonna need some backup," one of them called out.

"You think?" Barb replied.

"Chair!" They all ducked. A bright yellow bag chair—one of the deluxe models with two cup-holders and a canopy—flew overhead.

"Dude? Where'd that come from?" the youngest of them asked. He looked like Wally Cleaver.

"Jesus Christ." Barb sighed and walked to a pile of upended chairs. She carefully selected one, righted it, sat down, crossed her legs, fished her Zippo out of her shirt pocket, and proceeded to light up a smoke. The melee raged all around her. She shook her head. "This is like fucking Dodge City on a Saturday night."

Well, she thought, as she took another long drag off her cigarette, at least they got Tammy Faye Bakker off the microphone. She looked around. But where is that fucking music coming from?

She shrugged and settled back into her chair at the center of the maelstrom, smoking her Camel and listening to the hotel's lovely Muzak rendition of "The Girl From Ipanema."

Shawn and Kate bolted off the stage right after Cricket decided to use it as a launch pad and huddled behind a cluster of potted palms.

"What's happening now?" Kate asked.

A chair sailed by and crashed into a table loaded with glasses and pitchers of ice water.

"Shit!" Shawn tugged her closer. "I think this is what's called a good, old-fashioned brawl."

Kate ducked as a container of yogurt flew through the palm fronds above her head and landed with a splat on the floor behind them. "Does it occur to you that we never got a chance to answer a single question?"

"Yeah. It seems pretty clear that they didn't really need us for this shindig."

"Who knew?"

"I'm actually pretty relieved."

"You mean because we didn't have to disembowel each other on stage in front of fifteen hundred of our peers?"

"Shit!" Shawn clawed at something that had just dropped from the air and landed on her head. "What the fuck is this?" She pulled it off and held it up.

It was a bra. A very commodious bra.

Kate lifted up one of the cups. It was the size of a soup tureen. "Well. In case of a water evacuation, we could always use this as a lifeboat."

Shawn was mesmerized. "I think I'm in love."

Kate grabbed the garment out of her hands and tossed it back into the air. "One preoccupation at a time."

"Yes, dear."

"Do you have any ideas about how we can get the hell out of here?" Kate asked.

Shawn nodded. "I think there might be an exit over there behind the . . ."

"Behind the what?" Kate asked.

Shawn didn't answer. She was staring off into space with her mouth hanging open. Kate snapped her fingers. Twice. "Hello? Anybody home?"

Shawn looked at her. "Oh, you so won't believe this."

"What?"

"Look at what's headed our way." Shawn pointed at something over Kate's shoulder.

Kate twisted herself around so she could see what Shawn was talking about.

"Oh. My. God."

"Yeah."

"Please tell me she's not carrying who I think she's carrying."

Quinn Glatfelter was headed their way, and she had a woman slung over her shoulder like a hundred-pound sack of cornmeal.

"Is that Barbara Walters?" Shawn whispered.

Kate just nodded.

"Oh, god," Shawn said. "There goes that mainstream publishing contract."

Kate closed her eyes. It was too horrible to watch.

"There goes that GMA gig," she added.

Quinn was making a beeline for a service exit. She was nearly out of the room when she saw something that made her stop abruptly and turn around, her back to Shawn and Kate. Barbara Walters just hung there, calmly, with every hair still in place. She seemed almost relaxed—as if the fact that she was hanging upside down against the back of a BDSM butch biker was nothing out of the ordinary.

Quinn took two steps sideways and removed something that was dangling from a wall sconce, then she turned back around and continued on her way toward the service exit.

"What the hell did she pick up?" Shawn asked.

Kate squinted her eyes. "Oh, god."

"What?"

Kate looked at her. "It's that damn dog collar."

Shawn looked at her in horror. She looked back at the pair as they headed for the service door. Barbara Walters had pushed herself out away from Quinn's back and seemed to be studying something written on her t-shirt.

"Oh," Barbara Walters observed, as Quinn carried her past Shawn and Kate. "You use Astroglide?"

Two seconds later, the entire place erupted into an ear-splitting chorus of whistles and bullhorns.

The San Diego Police had arrived, and this party was coming to an end.

"That had to be a first date for the record books."

It was dark and quiet, and the only light in the room was coming from someplace down the hall.

Shawn leaned her forehead against Kate's. "I know."

"Never let it be said that you don't know how to show a lady a good time."

"I try my best."

Kate yawned. "I'm really beat."

"It's been quite a day."

Kate smiled. "It's been quite a damn year."

"Well," Shawn tried to pull her closer, "tie a knot and hang on, cause I don't think it's over yet."

"When are you going back to Charlotte?"

"Tuesday. After Gwen and I meet with Simon & Schuster in New York."

Kate shook her head. "I still can't believe that happened—especially after the riot."

"Well, to quote my mentor: 'I don't care what they say about me as long as they spell my name right.'"

"Barbara Streisand?"

"Nope."

"P.T. Barnum?"

"Nuh uh."

"Lady Gaga?"

"Not even close."

"Charlie the Tuna?"

Shawn drew back and looked at her in disbelief. "Charlie the Tuna? Seriously?"

Kate shrugged. "Okay. I give up."

"George M. Cohan."

"George M. Cohan? The annoying song and dance man?"

"That's the one."

"The Yankee Doodle Dandy guy?"

Shawn nodded.

"Oh, god." Kate threw back her head. "You really are a nerd, aren't you?"

"Yep. Think you can handle it? I mean, now that you're going to be this hot, T.V. star?"

Kate rolled her eyes. "I'm not hot, and I'm certainly not going to be a T.V. star."

"That's not what they're saying about you on TMZ."

"What are you talking about?"

"Viv told me that TMZ was sniffing around to get you to appear on an episode of *Women Behind Bars*."

"Viv told you this?"

Shawn nodded. "She also said that Barbara Walters was going to host it."

Kate shook her head. "Where does this woman get her information? She's got a faster network than Verizon."

"Still," Shawn said, "Barbara Walters ended up being a pretty class act."

"You can say that again. I never expected ABC to follow through with that weekend gig after what happened at the Con."

"Are you kidding? That video her cameraman shot went viral in about two seconds. ABC has had its highest ratings week in years."

"True."

"And having Ba-Ba wear a 'FREE THE C.L.I.T. CONS!' t-shirt on World News Tonight didn't hurt, either."

Shawn laughed. "Barb Davis said they'd sold enough of those to cover all of the damages to the hotel."

"I know. They even had enough coin left to purchase the rights to the riot video from ABC. It's already number one at the iTunes store."

Shawn laughed. "So. Is GMA gonna let you film your weekend segments in Atlanta?"

Kate gave Shawn a slow, sexy smile. "And anyplace else I might happen to be."

"Oh, really?" Shawn kissed her.

"Um hmmm. Anything going on in Charlotte that might be worth looking into?"

There was a loud metallic bang, and the dark room suddenly filled up with bright yellow light.

Moans and groans and cries of "What the fuck?" and "Turn off the goddamn lights," rose up around them. The big barred door at the front of their cell rolled back and locked into place with a thud so resounding it made the floor shake.

"Rise and shine, ladies," a big voice bellowed. "Come on . . . come on. Wake up." A nightstick rapped on the undersides of metal-framed cots. "Let's get it in gear, girls. You're outta here."

"Final-fucking-ly."

"Now you want us to leave? Why the hell didn't you let us go thirty-six damn hours ago?"

"I thought checkout time was at ten-thirty?"

"Shut up, Viv."

"Fuck you, Towanda. And get your stinky feet off my cot."

"Where's my damn bolo tie?"

"Anybody up for hitting that iHop we passed on the van ride when they brought us in here? I'm Jonesing for some pancakes."

"Stow the commentary." The big-bosomed matron was losing patience. "Just get your pampered dyke asses up and outta here. The WNBA is in town tonight, and we're gonna need this space."

"Hey?" Darien Black stood up and pulled on her leather jacket. "How'd we make bail?"

"Yeah," Viv chimed in. "That D.A. said we'd be cooling our heels in here for at least seventy-two hours."

"Right," Darien added. "The other twenty-eight brawlers who got arrested were charged and released in six damn hours."

The matron snorted. "You didn't make bail, honey, you just got lucky."

Kate and Shawn looked at each other.

"Lucky?" Shawn asked. "How, exactly, did we get lucky?"

"Let's just say that one of your girlfriends held the key." The matron laughed at her own joke. "The church key, if you get my drift."

Kate looked around the lockup. "Anybody seen V. Jay-Jay?"

"I'm over here," came a voice from outside the cell.

A baker's dozen of the world's bestselling lesbian authors turned in unison to look at V. Jay-Jay Singh, who calmly sauntered into their cell, sipping on a frosty Modelo.

"Where the hell have you been?" Towanda demanded.

"Now, now. Don't go looking a gift horse in the mouth, Wanda."

"Oh, good god . . ." Viv raised her eyes to the dingy ceiling. "Don't tell me that you got us out?"

V. Jay-Jay smiled sweetly at her. "You wanna tell them, Mavis?"

The big matron rolled her eyes.

"Every Friday night, the boys upstairs play poker. Every third Friday night, they play poker with the night shift crews from four other precincts."

Shawn knew where this was going. "Let me guess . . . this is the third Friday?"

Mavis nodded. "Yep. And the only thing them boys like more than playing cards is drinking beer. Lots and lots of beer."

"In bottles?" Kate asked.

Mavis shook her head. "Not usually. But tonight, Sgt. Koslovsky had six cases of designer shit in bottles left over from his daughter's wedding. There was just one problem."

"Oh, god." Kate closed her eyes.

"No opener?" Shawn asked.

"Until she showed up." Mavis pointed at V. Jay-Jay with her nightstick. "Crazy ass rug munchers."

"Ladies?" V. Jay-Jay lifted her leg and brought her foot down hard on the seat of a nearby wooden chair. A shower of metal bottle caps rained down on the floor. "Welcome to freedom."

Later that night, over coffee, cheese blintzes, and short stacks of pancakes, Vivien K. O'Reilly remarked that this was the first time V. Jay-Jay Singh ever got thirteen women off at the same time.

Thus was born the immortal legend.

The sisterhood clinked coffee mugs, knowing that future generations of lesbian authors would forever refer to them as "The CLIT-Con 13."

FALLING FROM GRACE

Going to a party was the last thing she felt like doing.

Well. Maybe having her fingernails pulled out one by one with rusty pliers would actually be the lastthing. But going to a party—any kind of party—had to be next in line right after that.

And a fucking costume party?

Even worse.

Who in the hell besides Annette Funicello threw a costume party to celebrate their sixtieth birthday?

Rizzo, that's who. Born on Halloween, and perpetually enamored of All Things Dead, Rizzo was famous for her macabre masked balls. And this year, she promised to make it one for the record books.

Yippee.

Grace sighed and looked out the tiny window next to her seat. She hadn't been anyplace in months. And this damn trip was costing her a fortune. But Rizzo was her best friend, and she had been planning this shindig for nearly a year. Long before Grace's relationship with Denise hit the skids.

Hit the skids? Hell. Roared off a goddamn cliff was more like it. You had to hand it to Denise. She didn't fuck around. When she decided that it was over, it was over. Capital O.

That was ten months ago. And those had been ten agonizing months for Grace. Ten months of trying to fit the broken shards of her life together into something that halfway resembled a human shape.

It was amazing. If you used enough duct tape and bailing twine, you could patch yourself up well enough to walk around without a limp. It was the ego that was harder to fix. And this time, it was a toss-up to determine which part of her took the biggest hit—her ego or her heart.

It had been a classic setup. An old standby. A golden oldie. A Blue Plate Special. One Number Six.

She got dumped for a younger woman.

And it got even better. She got dumped for a younger woman with an indifferent IQ, a head full of hair product, and a perky set of store-bought boobs.

But those were the breaks, right? The universe giveth, and the universe taketh away. The Ten Thousand Things rose and fell. And that was mostly okay—unless, of course, you happened to be the poor schmuck standing in the cross hairs when all Ten Thousand of the goddamn Things came crashing down to earth and nailed your ass.

There was a ding, and above her head, the fasten seatbelt light illuminated. They were coming into Phoenix. They had forty-five minutes on the ground, then the flight would continue on to San Francisco. She glanced at her watch. It wasn't really worth deplaning, and since she didn't have to change seats, she decided just to stay on the airplane and enjoy the solitude.

For once, the landing was uneventful. The flight was only half full, so it didn't take long for the rest of the passengers to collect their bags and head out into the heat. Grace leaned her head against the window frame and watched the bored-looking baggage handlers toss suitcases onto the conveyor like they were sacks of mulch.

It could always be worse, she thought. I could have to do that for a living.

Suddenly her job teaching English literature to bratty, self-important Millennials seemed like more of a gift than a curse.

"Excuse me, would you mind if I took this seat?"

Grace looked up to see a tallish woman wearing a tailored business suit standing in the aisle next to her row of seats. She was holding a book and a briefcase.

Grace stared at her stupidly for a moment before she realized that the woman was politely waiting for her to move her shit off the seat.

"God, I'm sorry," she said, collecting her notebooks and lesson plans. "Life at the center of the universe, you know?"

The tall woman smiled and sat down. "I apologize for disturbing you. I really wanted an exit row seat for the extra leg room, and all the other ones look taken." She gestured toward the seats across the aisle. They were filled with duffle bags or other personal belongings. "I thought I'd try to move up before they boarded the passengers for the next flight." She stowed her black leather briefcase under the seat ahead of her. It was a nice one. Monogrammed. "I guess we had the same idea," she added.

"What idea?" Grace asked.

"Staying on the plane during the layover?"

"Oh, that." Grace shrugged. "Ever been to Phoenix?"

The woman laughed. "Once—under duress. I swore I'd never do it again voluntarily."

"Wise woman. Unless, of course, you're into video games, in which case, you're missing a golden opportunity."

The woman pulled a small pair of reading glasses out of a sleeve inside her briefcase. "To do what?"

"I dunno. Win lots and lots of tokens that you can redeem for oddly-colored stuffed animals?"

"Unfortunately, I'm not much into stuffed animals. Nor am I very lucky, as a rule."

"That makes two of us."

The woman looked at her for a moment, and then extended her hand. "I'm Abbie."

Grace shook it. "Grace. Also unlucky at most games." And love, she thought.

"Where are you headed?"

Grace smiled at her. "Same place as you, I'd imagine."

"San Francisco?"

Grace nodded.

"Do you live there?"

Grace shook her head. "Nope. Never been there, in fact."

"Really? Is this a business trip?"

"No. Pleasure. I'm visiting an old friend."

"Same here."

"Small world."

"Sometimes it is." Abbie put on her glasses. For some reason, they made her look even more attractive. She glanced down at Grace's pile of papers. "Are you a teacher?"

Grace shrugged. "So they tell me."

"What do you teach?"

Grace sighed. "Right now, I'm teaching four sections of '*Beowulf* for Cretins.'"

Abbie laughed out loud. "I guess that's code for Freshman English?"

"You might say that."

"I think I just did."

"Oh really?" She tapped her fingers against her ear. "I must have a trace of tinnitus."

"From flying?"

"No, from straining to hear myself think."

Abbie smiled. "Are you sure you're not a night club comic?"

"Trust me," Grace replied. "No one would pay to listen to anything I have to say."

"Except maybe the parents of your cretins?"

"Oh they don't really have a choice."

"They don't?"

Grace shook her head. "Nope. For their kids, it's either college, or forced internment in a gulag."

Abbie raised an eyebrow. "Just where do you teach—Siberia?"

"Close. Ohio."

"Ah." Abbie glanced down at her feet. "That would explain the crampons."

Grace laughed. "Yes. I was amazed that TSA didn't confiscate them."

"Well, things have grown slack since the tenth anniversary of 9/11."

"So true." Grace looked at her. Damn. With her pulled-back dark hair, intelligent gray eyes, and killer smile, the woman really was gorgeous. She was probably in her late forties—classy, stylish. A great set of legs.

And totally out of her league.

Probably married.

When she could, she stole a glance at her ring finger.

Fuck. There it was—the inevitable band of gold.

It figured.

"Well," she said. "I suppose I should let you do whatever it was you intended to do when you decided to remain on the plane."

Abbie looked down at the book on her lap.

Grace followed her gaze. It was a bookmarked copy of Boccaccio's *De Mulieribus Claris. Jesus Christ.* So she was brilliant, too. Why was the universe so unkind?

"I suppose so." Abbie sounded almost disappointed. "I'm sorry. I'm not normally such a chatterbox."

"Oh, please." Grace extended a hand. "Don't apologize. I thought I was distracting you."

"Well, if you were, it was a distraction I welcomed."

They smiled at each other a little awkwardly. Like teenagers who had just been introduced at a sock hop.

A flight attendant who was making her way up the aisle from the rear of the aircraft stopped next to their row of seats.

"Would either of you ladies like something to drink?"

Grace looked up at her in surprise. "Can you do that?"

The flight attendant made a grand display of looking over both shoulders. "As long as you don't tell anyone," she whispered.

Grace looked at Abbie. "Do you drink?"

Abbie nodded. "Whenever possible."

"Okay," Grace said. "Bring us two of your most indifferent, over-priced wines."

The attendant smiled and nodded. "Red or white?"

"Red," they replied simultaneously.

The attendant continued on toward the front galley of the airplane.

"Wow." Grace shook her head. "I think my tinnitus is worse. I'm hearing echoes now."

"That wasn't an echo, it was an affirmation."

"Oh. No wonder I didn't recognize it."

"Really? I guess it's contagious."

"You, too?"

Abbie nodded. "It hasn't been one of my better years. But I think things are looking up."

"Short term, or long term?"

"If I'm lucky, maybe both."

"I thought you said you weren't lucky?" Grace smiled at her.

"I figure that sooner or later, the law of averages has to catch up with me."

"True," Grace said. "And failing that, there are rumored to be certain drug therapies that are efficacious."

"You mean, at producing medically-induced delusions?"

131

Grace nodded. "Of course. It's all the rage."

Abbie sighed. "Nobody tells me anything."

"Maybe you need to get out more?"

"Maybe I do."

Grace was about to reply when the flight attendant approached them with a tray containing two plastic cups of wine.

"Here you go, ladies. On the house." She handed them each a cup.

Grace looked up at her in surprise. "Really?"

"Yep. It looks like we're gonna be stuck here for a bit longer than forty-five minutes. There are some bad storms rolling through the Bay Area, and they've pushed our departure back."

Abbie looked concerned. "Do we need to get off the airplane?"

The flight attendant shook her head. "Not unless you get drunk and start swinging from the overhead bins." She smiled at them. "Enjoy the wine." She walked off.

Grace looked at Abbie. "I love Southwest."

Abbie held up her cup, and they clinked rims. "Me, too."

Grace discreetly looked her beautiful companion up and down. *Might as well torture myself a little more.* "So, if it's not too personal, why have you had such a bad year?"

Abbie flexed the fingers on her left hand and stared at her lap for a moment without answering.

"I'm sorry," Grace apologized. "I didn't mean to make you uncomfortable."

Abbie met her eyes. "No. It's okay. I'm not uncomfortable because of your question, I'm uncomfortable because of my answer."

"That's intriguing."

"Is it? Funny. From where I sit, it just feels pathetic."

"Well, why not just put it out there and let me judge for myself?"

Abbie seemed to think about that.

"All right. Why not?" Abbie set her cup of wine down on the tray table and half turned in her seat so she could cross her legs. Grace had to fight not to stare at them. *They really were things of beauty.*

"I lost my husband to heart disease eighteen months ago, and I've been struggling with how his death should change the way I live. That's really what this trip is about for me—figuring things out. Making choices."

Grace was stunned, and moved, by Abbie's honesty. She struggled with how to respond. "I can't imagine why you'd find that pathetic?"

"Ah. That's because you don't know what the choices are."

"Fair enough." Grace shook her head. "And I thought I was on god's shit list because I have to go to a damn costume party."

Abbie smiled at her. "'Tis the season, I suppose."

"That it is."

"What's your costume?"

Grace raised an eyebrow. "You don't really expect me to tell you, do you?"

Abbie shrugged. "I don't see why not. I more or less just showed you what's lurking behind mine."

"You're wearing a costume?"

"Of course. That's why my choices are complicated."

"I begin to see now why you wanted to be seated in the exit row."

"Do you?"

Grace felt her pulse rate accelerate. "I'm not really sure what we're talking about."

"Choices. Costumes." Abbie smiled. "And emergency exits."

Grace was beginning to feel like she needed to make use of one, before she made a fool of herself.

"Right. Okay. I'm going as a Greek philosopher."

"Which one?"

Grace held up her hands. "Take your pick."

"They're really not interchangeable."

"They are when you shop at Party City."

Abbie laughed.

"But since you asked, I was thinking about Demosthenes."

"An interesting choice. Why?"

"Because to pull it off, I only need a toga and a mouthful of pebbles. It greatly simplified packing for this trip."

"But won't the pebbles make it difficult to talk?"

Grace nodded with enthusiasm. "See? I knew you'd get it."

Abbie rolled her eyes. "Cheater."

"Not really. I hate talking to strangers."

Abbie sucked in her cheek.

Grace blushed. "I mean, generally."

Abbie took a sip from her cup of wine. "Lucky me."

Grace sighed as her pulse rate took off again.

They both looked up when the flight attendant appeared again.

"Drink up, ladies. It looks like there was a break in the weather action, and we're going to start boarding in a few minutes. I'll be back shortly to collect your cups." She walked on toward the rear of the aircraft.

Grace and Abbie looked at each other.

Grace held up her cup. "How about a toast?"

"Okay." Abbie followed suit.

"To having what we do become one with who we are."

Abbie stared at her for a moment before slowly clinking rims. "You really are eloquent—pebbles, notwithstanding."

"Only on Mondays and Wednesdays, from nine-oh-five to ten-ten."

Abbie looked at her watch. "It's ten-thirty, and today is Friday."

"It is?" Grace looked at her own watch. "Well holy Grendel's Mother."

"I guess nobody tells you anything, either?"

"You got that right, sister."

They finished their wine just as the first passengers started to board. As she fastened her seatbelt, Grace decided that maybe flying out for this party wasn't such a bad idea, after all.

Rizzo's birthday shindig was being held at the South End Rowing Club on Jefferson Street—a landmark in the Fisherman's Wharf neighborhood and a stone's throw from the Fort Mason cultural arts complex. It was a perfect venue for a party, with beautiful views of the Golden Gate and Bay Bridges, and a cavernous, wind-sheltered sundeck.

Rizzo promised that the guest list would be small—only twenty or thirty people—and she further insisted that Grace wouldn't have to worry about blending in because everyone would be in costume.

Right.

But when Rizzo insisted, it was best just to capitulate and go along. She'd learned that one the hard way. Rizzo was hardcore. A tough-talking, straight-shooting, don't-blow-smoke-up-my-ass, truth-teller who had survived more horrors than the combined casts of a dozen Brian de Palma movies.

You didn't say "no" to Rizzo. Not without a good goddamn reason—and, in this case, Grace didn't have one. A candy-ass case of ennui just didn't count.

So here she was, feeling short and ridiculous in her blue-trimmed toga and sandals.

At least the damn outfit was uncomplicated. Some of the other ensembles on display were fantastic, jaw-dropping creations right out of an Edith Head catalog. Rizzo, herself, was unadorned. She insisted that, as the hostess and guest of honor, she had the prerogative to appear however she fucking well chose.

Nobody argued with her.

She worked the room like a pro and made certain that everyone felt welcome, and that every empty hand was quickly filled with a fresh drink or a plate of hot food.

And she kept a watchful eye on Grace, making certain that she didn't drift off to any dark corners to brood or to hide from the rest of the crowd.

She knew Grace pretty well.

"Warner," she'd say. "Get over here. I want you to meet some people."

So she did. Countless people. A slew of names without faces, since most of them were wearing masks, or sporting so much cheap makeup it would be impossible to pick them out of a police lineup.

Maybe that was the point. Rizzo's guest lists tended to be pretty eclectic.

Later on, when the live music started, Grace seized the opportunity to sneak off the sundeck and meander down toward the water, where a flotilla of long boats was tied up in the small marina, and sea lions lazed about on the piers. The sun was setting, and the air rolling in across the bay was growing a lot colder. She knew she wouldn't be able to stay out here for very long. Her cheesy toga was too lightweight to offer much protection from the night air.

It really was beautiful. She could understand why Rizzo loved it here. Maybe she needed to make a change—get the hell out of Ohio and start over someplace new? Why not? There was nothing holding her there. Not now. Especially not her career. She liked her teaching job well enough. But colleges like Welles were a dime-a-dozen—self-important bastions of the liberal arts that offered upper-middle class white kids ivy-covered halls, small classes, and boutique majors—all for an annual tuition bill that would dwarf the sticker price on any new Lexus.

Change? Change could be a good thing. Why not move on and try to reinvent herself? She was still young enough to make a fresh start. She was . . .

Wasn't she?

135

"I thought that was you."

Grace was so startled by the voice coming from just behind her that she nearly dropped her glass of wine. It sloshed all over her hand and splattered across the front of her toga.

"Shit!" She shook her hand off to try and disperse the red liquid.

"Oh, god, I'm sorry." The voice was closer now.

Grace turned around to see that it was coming from . . . Bonnie Parker?

At least, she thought it was Bonnie Parker. The toy Tommy gun, the tweed suit, and the black beret were pretty big clues.

She looked lethal. And she looked hot as hell. In fact, she looked a lot like . . . Abbie.

"No way," Grace said, looking her up and down. "Is that really you?"

Abbie smiled. "I think so. Small world, isn't it?"

"You know Rizzo?" Grace was stunned.

Abbie nodded. "We met in grad school at Chicago, about a hundred years ago. But we've always stayed in touch. I wouldn't miss a big event in her life like this one—not for the world."

"I think I'm in shock."

"I know what you mean. I saw you about thirty minutes ago, shortly after I arrived, and I've been trying to make my way over to you to say hello. But by the time I finally broke free from some other college pals, you had disappeared. I came outside to see the view, and saw you down here." She gestured back toward the cook shack. "Frankly, I was also trying to escape the music."

Strains of "Now That I Found You" drifted toward them.

Grace struggled to avoid the irony. "Not a big fan of bluegrass?" she asked, with a smile.

Abbie shrugged. "I can tolerate the instrumental parts, but the vocals make my teeth hurt."

Grace stared at her for a moment, then shook her head. "I just can't believe we're both standing here at the same damn party. What are the odds?"

"I don't know." Abbie looked smug. "I think I told you that the law of averages would catch up with me sooner or later."

"I thought you were talking about wanting your luck to change?"

Abbie smiled at her. "That's exactly what I was talking about."

"I'm not trying to be dense, but how on earth does this qualify?"

"Do you always underestimate yourself?"

Grace was completely flustered. She had no idea how to respond, so she didn't make any response. She just stood there. Stupidly.

Abbie gestured toward the front of her toga. "I'm so sorry I startled you, now you've got red wine stains all over the front of your costume."

Grace looked down at it. "That's okay. If anyone asks, I'll just tell them I'm Julius Caesar."

Abbie laughed. "Beware the Ides of March?"

Grace nodded. "Maybe my luck will change, too?"

"Maybe it already has."

They stared at each other again.

"I'm not sure if . . . are you . . . ?" Grace didn't know how to finish her question.

"Am I what?"

How was it possible for Abbie to be so goddamn calm? "Just exactly what kind of life changes are you talking about making?"

Abbie hefted the barrel of her Tommy gun before resting it against her shoulder. "I don't know. Maybe I'll embrace a life of crime."

"That's one way to blaze a trail."

"Or maybe I'll embrace something else."

"Such as?"

Abbie shrugged.

"Losing your courage?" Grace asked.

"On the contrary," Abbie replied. "I think I'm finding it."

Grace could feel her pulse rate going haywire again.

"What are we really talking about, Abbie?"

"You're a friend of Rizzo's. You shouldn't have to ask me that."

"Rizzo isn't gay."

"No. But you are."

Grace narrowed her eyes. "Does my toga zip on the wrong side or something?"

"Not that I can tell," Abbie replied, looking her over.

"Then how in the hell would you know something like that about me?"

"Am I wrong?"

"I didn't say that."

Abbie smiled. "Maybe I asked."

"You asked about me?"

Abbie nodded.

"Why?"

Abbie rolled her eyes.

"No. Come on . . . you said you were married."

"I was married."

Grace still didn't get it. "And now?"

"Now I'm not married."

"But you're curious?"

"Not exactly."

"You're not curious?"

"Well, curious about you, maybe. But not about this."

Grace sighed. "I think I need another drink."

Abbie smiled. "I can take care of that. Wait right here."

Grace touched her on the arm. "Gimme the gun. I'll cover you."

Abbie laughed and handed it over to her. "I didn't know this was hostile territory."

"You can't be too careful."

Abbie met her eyes. "Believe me when I tell you that you can."

"Is that what this is about?"

"No. This is about getting you some more wine." Abbie laid a hand on Grace's forearm. "And maybe a jacket. You're freezing. Stay put. I'll be right back."

Grace watched her walk back toward the cook shack. She was wearing a knit sweater and a tight tweed skirt. She looked a lot more like Faye Dunaway than Bonnie Parker.

Not that anyone would complain about that. The woman was hot.

Holy shit. This is so not happening, Grace thought. The last thing I need right now is to become somebody's goddamn science experiment.

Abbie reached the steps that led up to the sundeck and turned around and waved.

On the other hand, why the hell not? It's not like we'll ever run into each other again.

They spent the next hour, sitting on a bench overlooking the water, watching the flicker of lights on the two bridges.

Grace learned a little bit more about Abbie. A very little bit. She lived in North Carolina, and had been married for six years before her husband died. They had no kids. For the last two years, she'd worked as the executive director of a nonprofit philanthropic group. She liked the work, but felt that she was ready for something different.

Grace wondered if her desire for something different helped explain why she was spending the better part of the evening sitting on a bench in the cold and trading witticisms with a stranger.

It was clear to her by now that Abbie was flirting with her—testing the waters. Hell. There was enough electricity flying back and forth between them to light up one of those fucking bridges.

So what was she going to do about it? It couldn't go anyplace. That much was clear. They lived in different parts of the country, and for all practical purposes, she knew next to nothing about her.

But none of that mattered. That wasn't what this was about. This was about something that Grace rarely did, and hadn't done in over ten years. This was about what Rizzo liked to call "an overnight rental," or at least it could be, if she played her cards right and didn't lose her nerve.

She shivered. The breeze off the water was like a blast from an open freezer door.

"You're cold." Abbie shifted closer to her on the bench. Grace didn't mind.

"It's my own fault for picking such a ridiculous costume. I should've gone with my first choice."

"Which was?" Abbie asked.

Grace looked at her. "Scooby Doo."

Abbie laughed.

"You find that amusing?"

She nodded. "It's hard to imagine you dressed up like a giant dog."

"I don't see why? It would have had several advantages."

"Like?"

Grace held up her hand and commenced ticking the advantages off on her fingers. "Well, first, there's the fur coat."

Abbie nodded. "I can see where that would have been beneficial."

"Second, there's the flea collar. Very useful when you're traveling in warmer climates."

Abbie looked dubious. "Okaaayyy."

"Third, it would have allowed me to do things that I could never do dressed like this."

Abbie looked intrigued . . . and suspicious. "Is that a fact?"

"Oh, yes. Absolutely."

"What kinds of things, exactly?"

"Oh, you know . . . dog kinds of things."

"Dog kinds of things?"

"Yeah."

"And what might those be?"

Grace had no idea where her newfound bravado was coming from, but she decided to run with it. "Do you need me to show you?"

Abbie took a long, slow breath. Jesus, the woman was sexy as hell.

"I'll probably live to regret this, but, yes. Show me."

Grace took hold of Abbie's face with both hands. Her skin felt soft and warm. With the small part of her brain that was thinking rationally, she wondered how it was possible for Abbie to be so goddamn warm when she was fighting to keep her own hands from shaking. As slowly as she could, she leaned forward until their faces were nearly touching. Abbie remained completely still and made no effort to pull away. Their breath mingled on the night air as Grace hovered there. Then, in a flash, she stuck out her tongue and licked the tip of Abbie's nose. Just as quickly, she dropped her hands and sat back against the bench.

"That kind of thing," she said.

Abbie looked incredulous. "Did you just lick me on the nose?"

Grace nodded.

"I can't believe you did that," she said.

"Why not? You asked me to show you."

Abbie shook her head. "All I can say is, thank god you didn't get the Scooby Doo costume."

"That bad, huh?"

"I'll say."

"I guess it was a lame joke." Grace touched her on the arm. "I'm really sorry."

Abbie looked at her. In the half light, her eyes glowed like hot coals. "I'm not." Her voice sounded husky.

Grace's head was starting to spin. "I'm confused again. You're not sorry?"

"Not at all. If you were dressed like a dog I couldn't do this."

Before Grace knew what was happening, Abbie closed the distance between them and kissed her. Hard.

Grace had been kissed before, but never quite like this. There was something raw and uncontrolled in the way they came together. The kiss went on and on. Grace was practically in her lap by the time they finally broke apart.

"Woof," she said when she could find her voice.

Abbie laughed softly against her hair.

"As soon as I can manage to stand up, I want you to push me into the bay."

Abbie drew back. "Why on earth would I do that?"

"Too cool my ass off," Grace said.

"I thought you were already cold?"

Grace shook her head. "Not anymore."

Abbie pulled her closer. "Maybe I like having you hot."

Okay. There was that pulse rate thing again. "I think we should talk about this."

Abbie kissed across her forehead. "Really? Talking is what you want to do right now?"

Grace swallowed hard and forced herself to draw back. "Of course not. What I want is a whole lot more related to . . . nonverbal communication."

Abbie smiled and reached for her again. "Me, too."

Grace held up a hand. "Wait. I haven't done this in a really long time." She paused. "Well . . . I mean . . . I haven't done this, not in this way."

Abbie looked confused. "I know I've been out of circulation for a while, but how many ways are there to do it?"

"That isn't what I meant."

"All right. What did you mean?"

Grace took a deep breath. "How about I ask you a question instead?"

"Okay." Abbie sat back and folded her arms.

"You've been with women before?"

Abbie thought about that. "Define 'been with.'"

"You're really going to make me work for this, aren't you?"

Abbie gave her a shy smile. "I'm sorry. I don't mean to be obtuse. This isn't something I have much experience talking about."

Grace nodded. "Well, here's your opportunity to practice."

"Funny you should say that. I thought that's exactly what I was doing."

Grace laughed. "Honey, if that's what you call practice, then you're a shoo-in for a reserved seat at the head of the class."

Abbie smiled. "I've always been an overachiever."

Grace smiled, too. "Lucky me."

They stared at each other for a moment without speaking. Behind them, the band's spirited rendition of Willie Nelson's "Gotta Get Drunk" finished with a flourish, and a wave of applause rolled out across the small marina. Grace heard the bandleader thank the audience. It seemed clear that the entertainment portion of the party was over. That meant that Rizzo would be making her rounds again. They probably didn't have much more time to sit here, alone in the dark.

Fuck me, and my damn scruples for wasting it. Women like Abbie sure as shit didn't come her way very often.

What the hell was she thinking? Women like Abbie never came her way.

She sighed and nodded toward the lighted patio behind them. "I think we just ran out of time."

Abbie followed her gaze, then looked back at Grace. "Maybe not."

Grace raised an eyebrow.

"Where are you staying?"

Something fluttered inside her chest. "The Fairmont in Ghirardelli Square."

Abbie smiled. "Me, too."

"I had a coupon," she explained.

Abbie shook her head. "Are you walking?"

Grace nodded.

"Me, too." She glanced at her watch. "Want to meet me out front in about thirty minutes?"

Grace nodded again.

"Are you okay?" Abbie touched her hand.

"I honestly don't know. I feel like I'm sleepwalking."

"Funny. I feel like I'm finally starting to wake up."

"What the hell are you two doing out here?" Rizzo's voice cut through the darkness. "Come on back up here. We're getting ready to do the cake."

Grace turned around to see their hostess leaning over the railing of the sundeck. She was framed by the backlight of a hundred Japanese lanterns. Her shape was unmistakable, and so was her air of authority.

"Save me a corner piece," Grace called out to her.

"Fuck you. Come get it yourself." Rizzo turned around and disappeared into the crowd.

Grace looked at Abbie and sighed. "She has such a way with words."

Abbie agreed. "I know. It's a useful skill for a poet."

They shared a laugh, then stood up, and slowly made their way back to the party. They reached the wooden steps to the sundeck, and Abbie linked her index finger with Grace's. For some reason, it felt like the most erotic thing she'd ever experienced.

She looked at Abbie. "Did you say thirty minutes?"

Abbie nodded and smiled.

I'll eat fast."

Abbie gave her finger a short squeeze, and then released it when they reached the top step. They separated and rejoined the party.

Three-hundred-and-twenty-four bucks was the most she'd ever spent on a hotel room—especially one she never used.

Grace unlocked the door with her keycard and stepped inside. It was freezing in here. The AC was blasting. She forgot that she'd set it so low before she left for the party last night.

She leaned against the back of the big door and closed her eyes.

Good god. Did any of that really happen?

It was so not who she was.

But wasn't that what they'd each talked about wanting to do? Change who they were?

Right. Who they were, but not how they lived. Today, they each were headed back to their real lives. Alone. Abbie was already on her way to the airport. Her flight for Raleigh was leaving in an hour.

They made no promises, and no offers to stay in touch. Abbie never suggested it, and Grace didn't have the courage to offer first. So they both remained silent.

It was a missed opportunity. She knew it. One she'd probably keep on missing for the rest of her life.

Christ. She didn't even know her last name.

So now, she'd collect her shit and head back to Ohio with nothing more than a memory.

Unless . . . She could always ask Rizzo about Abbie.

No. If Abbie had wanted to stay in touch, she'd have said so. They would have exchanged names and phone numbers. They'd have talked about finding ways to try and meet again in one place or the other.

But Abbie said nothing, so Grace said nothing.

Fuck it. Grow up. You knew what you were doing. Don't weep about it now. There are no victims in this little drama.

She sighed and walked to the bed and flopped down. She had four hours to kill until her flight left. Might as well try to get a little sleep, since she didn't get any last night.

She closed her eyes, but all she could see were visions of Abbie.

Jesus. The woman sure made up for lost time. They both did. It was fantastic. Incredible. Without a doubt, it was the most erotic and exciting thing she'd ever done. What Abbie seemed to lack in experience, she made up for with enthusiasm, and determination. And she wasn't kidding. She was one hell of a fast learner. In fact, Grace had felt like the novice. *What a great problem to have.*

She rolled over and stared at the bedside clock.

This was a colossal waste of time. She was too keyed-up to sleep. Only one thing could help her now. She got up to head for the bathroom and a cold shower.

Back at Welles, things soon settled back into a normal routine. Memories of her overnight rental didn't exactly fade, but they slowly became easier to think about without an accompanying attack of angst. Or regret. She resolved to chalk the entire experience up to a growth spurt—an exponential leap forward in her recovery from the Disaster-That-Was-Denise.

Classes were winding down in advance of the Thanksgiving holiday. All four sections of her English Lit survey had papers due. She'd be up to her ass in reams of bad prose by Tuesday afternoon. She knew better than to waste her time holding classes on Wednesday. The students would all have decamped for home long before then.

The semester would be over soon. Then the long Christmas break would give her a chance to work on her book. That was how she filled up the empty spaces in her life right now—by resurrecting her ill-fated attempt at writing the next Great American Novel.

Well, it wasn't really so great, but at least it kept her busy through the succession of dull and interminable nights that kicked in after Denise moved out.

She sat down in front of her office computer to check her e-mail one last time before packing up and heading for home.

There were several messages from students offering creative excuses for why their papers would be late. She archived those for later. There were also two messages marked "high priority" from the Presidential Search Committee. One suggested that an announcement from Trustees would be forthcoming soon. The second was actually from the Board Chair—inviting the entire community to an all-campus meeting at two o'clock that afternoon.

Grace looked at her watch.

Fuck. She wanted to get a jump on holiday traffic herself and head out for her parents' farm in Pennsylvania before it started getting dark. But now she'd be stuck here with everyone else. There was a follow-up e-mail from her department chair that stated that all members of the English faculty who were still on campus would be expected to attend the announcement.

Not that she would want to miss it. An event like this one was a big deal in the life of a small college. The last two presidents of Welles had been pulled from business backgrounds. This time, the faculty was hopeful that they'd get a real academic at the helm—someone who would take a greater interest in curricular development and scholarship, rather than shaking the money tree.

She sighed. Fat chance. It was all about raising money these days. Still . . . it would be interesting to see which one of their dried-up old clones the big boys flushed out this go-round.

She shut down her computer and picked up her backpack. She'd have just enough time to run home and grab a sandwich before the meeting. She got outside and saw, with a sinking feeling, that it had started to snow. And it was already sticking. Great. The drive to Pennsylvania in the dark should be a real blast.

The auditorium was packed.

And things were definitely looking up. Grace exchanged surprised glances with Tom Shepard as the board chair finished talking about the methodology used by the search committee and finally shared details from the Chosen One's curriculum vitae.

It slowly became clear that, this time, the committee had actually listened to the faculty. The new president was an academic with a solid background in research and scholarly publication—a teacher and a thinker with stellar credentials, including an undergraduate degree from Dartmouth, and a Ph.D. in History from the University of Chicago. The winning candidate had authored a list of books and articles half a mile long, had served for six years as a full professor and associate vice president at Duke, and had two years of executive experience directing the Z. Smith Reynolds Foundation—one of the largest, private endowments in the country.

It was a slam dunk, and the board chair knew it. The normally unimpressed members of the Welles faculty were literally sitting on the ends of their seats, waiting for the big reveal. You could've heard a pin drop in that joint.

He made them wait.

"When she joins us on January fifteenth, we will begin a new chapter in the life of this exceptional institution of higher learning," he said.

Tom and Grace looked at each other in shock. *She?*

An audible titter of conversation spread across the hall.

The board chair smiled. "No, that wasn't a mistake. I said 'she.'"

The hall erupted in applause. People got to their feet.

The chair shouted over the din, "It gives me great pleasure to introduce the twenty-second President of Welles College, Elizabeth Abbott Williams."

The applause in the hall was deafening. People were whooping and cheering. Grace got to her feet and strained to see around the bobbing rows of heads in front of her.

The cheers and the applause went on and on. This was a seminal event in the life of this college—the first female president in its two-hundred-and-twenty-year history.

Grace finally took a step out into the aisle so she could get a glimpse of their new leader, who had taken the stage and now stood towering over the board chair, smiling and nodding at the audience. Grace stared, stunned, and dropped back into her seat.

Jesus H. Christ.

Her hands were shaking. She felt light-headed and feared she might pass out. She knew that Tom was looking at her strangely.

This was not happening.

It was Abbie.

Grace's mother was pissed when she called to tell her that she hadn't been able to leave because of a last-minute, mandatory faculty meeting—and that it now was snowing so hard she didn't think she'd be able to make the long drive to the farm that night.

"I'll try in the morning," she said. But she knew she probably wouldn't. Even if the snow didn't amount to much. It wasn't supposed to. The big system that had been wreaking havoc in the northern plains all week was still inching its way across the country, but it wouldn't reach Ohio until the first of the week at the earliest.

The truth was, Grace just didn't have the focus or stamina to attempt the trip. Not now. Not after seeing Abbie.

Correction. Not after seeing the new president of Welles—her boss.

God.

It was like some kind of twisted Eugene O'Neill play. A ludicrous joke—and she was the punch line. These things didn't happen in real life. These things only happened in literature to characters like Oedipus—or in movies to actors like Deborah Kerr.

What the hell was she supposed to do now? Pack up and move to Idaho?

She scoffed and took another big swig from the Grey Goose bottle. It had been part of a thank-you goodie basket sent to her from members of the curriculum committee she'd chaired all semester.

Pear-flavored vodka. How . . . inventive. It was only a pint bottle, but right now, it was getting the job done just fine.

She was sitting on the back steps of her small house. The snow was still coming down. Big, wet flakes that stuck to every surface—including her. She knew that her jacket and her hair were covered, but she didn't really care. Maybe if she sat here long enough, she'd blend right into the landscape, and she'd never have to worry about how Abbie would react when she finally noticed her.

"What the hell is the matter with you?" Tom Shepard had asked earlier, as he caught up with her outside the auditorium after the announcement. "And why are you walking so goddamn fast?"

Grace just shook him off. "I don't feel so well. I think it must've been those hot dogs I ate at the Commons."

He looked skeptical. "You ate hot dogs at the Welles cafeteria? Is this some new self-flagellation technique?"

"Could be." She didn't want to prolong the conversation. "Look, Tom, I really feel sick." It wasn't far from the truth.

"Oh, man." He ran a hand through his short Afro. "I really wanted to talk about this. Call me later?"

She shrugged. "Maybe."

She veered off on a brick sidewalk that led away from Ames Hall, where the English department offices were located. "See you after the break, okay?"

He continued to stand there as she walked away. "Hey, Grace?"

She stopped and turned around.

"She's pretty hot, isn't she?" He winked at her. "Just your type, too."

Grace hadn't really eaten any hot dogs that day, but right then, she really felt like throwing up.

"Yeah," she said, turning away. Snow was pelting her in the face. It felt like it had bits of sleet in it. "She's just my type."

Christ. She took another drink. Once the vodka was gone she knew she'd start feeling how fucking cold it was out here.

The nine o'clock dog was barking.

Every twelve hours at precisely nine o'clock, her neighbor's dog barked—without fail. In rain, sleet, or snow—on the brightest of days, or the darkest of nights—if it was nine o'clock, Grendel barked. The nine o'clock dog was one of the constants in her life—just like grading papers, watching reruns of Frasier, or meeting the wrong goddamn women.

She checked her watch. Yep. Nine o'clock. Straight up.

She raised the bottle in a toast. "More power to ya, Grendel. If I had the chops, I'd be barking, too."

But Grendel wasn't paying any attention to her. Grendel was frantically pacing back and forth along the fence that flanked her yard. This was a much more vigilant display than usual, and she was barking well beyond the requirements of her customary alert. Clearly, someone was coming to kill them all, and Grendel didn't understand why no one else seemed to care.

Grace didn't have the patience to try, either. She'd just about decided to get up and go inside when she caught sight of someone coming around the corner of the house.

Shit. Company was the last thing she needed. And who the hell would show up at this time of night the Wednesday before Thanksgiving?

A person, wearing a long black coat with a hood, stood there a moment in the swirling snow before advancing toward the porch. Grace felt a moment of panic. Maybe Grendel was right? Then the figure tossed back its hood.

The warm buzz she'd been feeling from the vodka evaporated in a nanosecond. It was Abbie. Again.

"Jesus Christ," she blurted. "You scared the shit out of me."

Abbie stopped in front of her. Her expression was ominous—like a reflection of the storm. "Now . . . or earlier today?"

Grace shrugged. "Take your pick."

"Can I sit down?"

"Can I stop you?"

Abbie sighed. "You can if you want to."

Grace hesitated.

"I guess showing up here was a bad idea," Abbie said.

"Now—or earlier today?" Grace quoted.

"Very funny."

"I do try."

"I remember."

"How did you find me?" Grace asked.

Abbie shrugged.

Grace gave a bitter laugh. "I guess rank has its privileges."

"I saw you from the stage."

"You did?"

Abbie nodded. "I was stunned."

"That makes two of us."

Grendel was still barking.

"You might as well come inside," Grace said. "She'll never stop if we stay out here."

"Would that be okay? My feet are freezing."

Grace looked down at her shoes. "You walked here in those?"

"I didn't exactly plan on hiking through the snow when I got dressed this morning."

Grace nodded. "Shit happens."

"That's true."

Abbie stared over her shoulder at the barking dog, which was standing up on its hind legs and leaning against the fence. She looked back at Grace. "Its tail is wagging."

"She's conflicted." Grace shrugged. "It's going around."

Abbie actually smiled. She gestured at the bottle Grace was holding. "What are you drinking?"

Grace held it up. "This? It's pear-flavored vodka."

Abbie made a face. "I think I'll pass."

"Wise decision."

"Got anything else?"

Grace stood up and opened the door so Abbie could enter the house. "Only one way to find out."

They went inside. Grace kicked off her shoes, then removed her soggy jacket and hung it up on a hook near the door. She turned to Abbie. "May I take your shroud?"

Abbie rolled her eyes. "Sure." She shrugged out of her long coat and handed it to Grace.

They were standing in a small, glassed-in porch that overlooked Grace's back yard. It was simply furnished with several distressed-looking Adirondack chairs that were painted in bold colors and a faded outdoor rug. A tower of papers stood on a table next to one of the chairs.

"This is a great porch," Abbie said. "You must spend a lot of time out here."

Grace nodded. "I try to. It takes some of the sting out of all the hours I spend grading papers."

"I can imagine."

"That's right. You've done your time in the classroom, too, haven't you?"

Abbie shrugged.

"Don't be so modest, Dr. Williams."

Abbie looked at her. "You seem determined to make this harder than it already is."

"Define 'this.'" Grace made air quotes with her fingers.

"Our . . . predicament."

Grace folded her arms. "We have a predicament?"

"I'd say so."

Grace knew that she was acting like a bitch, and she needed to snap out of it. This mess wasn't Abbie's fault. It wasn't anybody's fault.

She took a deep breath. "I'm sorry. Take off your wet shoes and come on into the house where it's warmer."

Abbie took off her shoes and followed Grace into the kitchen. It was small, but cozy and well appointed.

"Have a seat." Grace indicated a small table and two chairs in the corner of the room. She walked to a tall cabinet and withdrew two glasses and a fat brown bottle. "Like cognac?"

Abbie nodded. "Got any coffee to go with it?"

"At nine o'clock at night?"

Abbie shrugged. "I don't think I need to worry about it keeping me awake."

"I see your point. I'll make us a fresh pot."

Abbie sat down and looked around the kitchen while Grace made the coffee. "How long have you been here?"

"Do you mean in this house, or at Welles?"

Abbie smiled at her. "Yes."

Grace carried the bottle and the two glasses to the table and sat down across from her. "Four years. I came up for tenure last year."

"And you got it."

"Yep." She poured them each a generous splash of cognac. "There's no accounting for taste."

"Well," Abbie picked up her glass, "you have to admit, it does simplify some things."

"Like?" Grace was intrigued.

"You're a tenured professor—that means there is less opportunity for conflict of interest concerns."

"You mean because you're my new boss?"

"Technically, I'm not your boss. I'm your boss's boss."

"Isn't that the same thing?"

Abbie shook her head. "Not really."

Grace twirled her glass around. "This is a mess."

"I know."

She met Abbie's incredible gray eyes. "I keep thinking about what Oscar Wilde said."

"What's that?"

Grace sighed. "That there are only two tragedies in life. One is not getting what you want, and the other is getting it."

"Which one is this?"

"You tell me."

"I'm not sure I know yet."

They sat in silence for a few moments. Grace could hear sleet hitting the kitchen window.

"I thought about trying to find you," Abbie said in a quiet voice. "More than once."

Grace put her glass down. She didn't really need anything else to drink. "Why didn't you?"

Abbie looked down at the tabletop. "I was a mess. I was confused. I didn't know what I wanted."

"And now?"

"Now? I'm still a mess—and I'm still confused." She raised her eyes. "But I think I know what I want."

Grace could feel her heart starting to pound. "You do?"

Abbie nodded. "But it's complicated."

Grace laughed out loud. "You think?"

Abbie smiled. "Did you ever think about trying to find me?"

"You're kidding, right?"

Abbie shook her head.

"Of course I did." She hesitated. "I nearly called Rizzo a dozen times. You know, I've never done anything like that before. It was . . . amazing."

"Yes. It was."

Grace waved a hand in frustration. "But you never said anything. You never asked me for my phone number—or even for my last name." She took a drink of the cognac. It went down her throat like liquid fire. She knew she'd pay for this tomorrow.

"I didn't think I could. I felt too . . . vulnerable. Too exposed and inexperienced."

"I'm sorry about that."

"No." Abbie laid a hand on top of Grace's. "Don't be. It was wonderful. You were wonderful."

Grace felt an increase of excitement and trepidation in nearly equal measure.

But this was impossible. There was no way for them to go forward from here.

She turned her hand beneath Abbie's over. "Did you know I worked here?"

"No." Abbie squeezed her fingers. "I had no idea. I was as shocked to see you as I'm certain you were to see me."

"How did you find me?"

Abbie shrugged. "After dinner with the trustees, I had a few minutes alone so I could peruse the English department web site. Once I found the profile for Grace Warner, I asked my assistant to get me your home address. I told her that we had friends in common, and that I had promised to look you up."

"Plausible."

"That's what I thought."

They lapsed into silence again, but they continued to sit there, holding hands. The coffeemaker beeped to signify that it had finished brewing, but they both ignored it. Abbie's fingers felt strong and solid. Grace was reminded of the time when she was ten, and had been horsing around on the farm with her brother. They had been playing on top of a partially-filled grain silo, and Grace had slipped and fallen into it. When her brother was unable to get her out, he panicked and ran off to get their father, who climbed down the bin ladder and rescued her. She remembered the relief she felt when she finally grabbed onto him. Right now, Abbie's hand felt the same way—like a sure and certain lifeline that could lift her out of this dark vat of professional quicksand.

She squeezed the fingers beneath hers. "What do you want?"

"Isn't it obvious?" Abbie replied.

Grace shook her head.

"I took this job—this particular job at Welles—because this appeared to be an open community . . . one that allows and encourages people to be who they are."

"That's true," Grace said. Before the Civil War, Welles had been a stop on the Underground Railroad. It had also been one of the first colleges in the country to admit students of color—and women. Grace had been an out lesbian the whole time she'd taught here—and it had never been an issue. Hell . . . it probably helped her get tenure.

"So you came here because you thought it would be a safe place to experiment with an alternative lifestyle?"

"No, Grace," Abbie said. "I came here because I wanted—finally— to have the latitude to be who I really am."

"And who is that?"

Abbie sighed. "You of all people should know the answer to that question."

"Abbie. I spent the better part of a day, and most of one incredible night with you, but I'd hardly say that qualifies me to know who you are."

Abbie slowly nodded her head. She started to withdraw her hand, but Grace held on to it.

"Not so fast," she said. "That doesn't mean I'm not interested in finding out."

Abbie's expression lost some of its sadness. "Really?"

Grace nodded.

They smiled somewhat shyly at each other.

"So," Grace asked, "how do we do this?"

Abbie shook her dark head. "Beats the hell outta me. I was hoping you'd have some ideas."

"Oh," Grace looked her up and down, "I have a few ideas all right."

Abbie smiled. "Not those kinds of ideas. However," she tugged Grace forward until their noses were nearly touching, "those certainly have some relevance to our . . . deliberations."

"You think so?"

"I know so." Abbie kissed her. It was just a quick, light kiss, but Grace could feel her toes curling up inside her socks.

"It's still sleeting," she said when she could find her voice.

"It is."

"And we have this whole pot of coffee."

"We do, indeed."

"We're two uncommonly smart women, aren't we?" Grace asked.

Abbie thought about it. "I'd say so. Between the two of us, we probably have about eight million years of post-graduate education."

"And in my case, twice that amount in unpaid student loans."

Abbie drew back and looked at her with a raised eyebrow. "I may need to rethink this idea."

"Nuh uh." Grace pulled her closer again. "Drop/Add day already came and went, sister. You're stuck in this little seminar until the bitter end."

"Oh really?" Abbie didn't sound too distressed by this revelation. "How will I know when we're finished?"

"Oh, that's easy." Grace took her face between both hands. "Just listen for the nine o'clock dog."

"The nine o'clock dog?"

"Don't worry." Grace kissed her. "It'll make sense soon enough."

154

Out back in the neighbor's yard, Grendel finally gave up her vigil for the night and retreated to the security of her doghouse. Morning would come soon enough, and with it, a host of new and unforeseen threats. For now, she could retire safely and rest while the landscape filled up with the calm and quiet that always accompanied an unexpected snow.

NEVERMORE!

"1-800-SPANK me. I know that number." Diz was staring at the caller I.D. readout on her cell phone.

Clarissa glanced at her. "You should. You practically have it on speed dial."

Diz snapped her phone shut and tossed a malted milk ball at Clarissa. Christmas was only a few days away, and the office break room was inundated with tins full of cheap confections from vendors.

It was a good throw. It landed in Clarissa's coffee, causing it to slosh all over the article she was proofreading.

"Oh, nice one, nimrod." Clarissa snatched up the top pages and shook them off over her waste can. "Great." She held up the top page. Spidery blue lines from what had been notes were running down the sheet of paper like varicose veins. "You can be such an asshole. Now I'll have to do this all over again."

Diz shrugged. "You impugn my integrity and then take umbrage when I defend myself?"

Clarissa sighed. "Eighteen people in this department, and I get to share a rabbit hutch with you. Someday I'm going to figure out who I pissed off in a previous life."

Diz snapped her bright red suspenders and stuck out her tongue.

"Oh, that's mature. And what's with the outfit today? You look like Howdy Doody on crack."

Diz rolled her eyes. "Give me a break, Clar. It's for the Christmas party. Besides, you wouldn't know Howdy Doody if he walked up and bit you on your high-class ass."

Clarissa opened her mouth to reply just as her phone rang. She turned away from Diz and snapped it up. "Research, this is Clarissa Wylie."

Diz watched her while she talked. She and Clarissa had been working together for nearly two years, now. They weren't exactly friends—not in the sense that they ever did much together socially. But that wasn't hard to understand. Clarissa came from money—old money. And her family owned the company that published the magazine they worked for. In fact, her family's company published half the goddamn magazines printed in the U.S.

Clarissa was a comer. Everybody knew that. Since finishing grad school at Princeton, she was paying her dues by working her way up through the ranks of the family business. One year in subscription services, eighteen months in distribution, and a whopping two years in research with Diz. Her next move would certainly be to a private office upstairs in the editorial suite. But you had to give her credit—she worked hard, and she knew her shit.

Diz, on the other hand, was pretty much fated to remain chained to her desk in the bowels of the building, vetting facts and making sure the Wylies didn't get sued for libel or plagiarism. That was okay. This was just her day job. At night, she slaved away on her other passion—a comprehensive and comparative study of the development of detective fiction as a literary genre. She was A.B.D.—all-but-dissertation—and after six years of night school, she was only nine hundred plus pages away from earning her doctorate in American literature from the University of Baltimore.

Dr. Gillespie—what a nice ring that had. Of course, she'd always be Diz to her family and friends. The childhood nickname started out as homage to her father's love of jazz, but it stuck. And frankly, it suited her a whole lot better than her given name.

And once she finally had that sheepskin, she'd blow this pop stand and . . . and what?

And be an unemployed Ph.D.

Oh, well. There were worse things. She could end up like her idol. Poe died alone in poverty at age forty, about five blocks away from this goddamn building.

She glanced at Clarissa, who was still talking. Correction, listening.

She was jotting notes down in longhand, using that damn, precious Italian fountain pen of hers.

Diz studied her. It wasn't the first time.

Clarissa wasn't just a comer, she was a looker, too. Her thick auburn hair cascaded down her back like a red waterfall. And she had a set of legs that would make Betty Grable's pale by comparison. She knew how to dress for them, too. Today she was wearing a form-fitting black suit and stylish shoes that probably cost more than Diz spent on clothing in a year. Correction—in five years. Although she admired the view, Diz wondered why Clarissa bothered. It wasn't like anyone who mattered was going to see her down here in this dank basement.

Clarissa turned her head and caught Diz staring. She frowned and tossed a paper clip at her. Diz caught it. Diz always caught anything Clarissa tossed at her, except compliments, of course. Diz usually let those fly by like fastballs that were thrown outside the strike zone. It was better for Diz not to indulge in how great it felt when Clarissa paid attention to her. That was one dead-end street that she just didn't need to travel. Everyone knew that Clarissa was A.B.E.—all-but-engaged. And her intended was the granite-jawed, heir-apparent to Baltimore's oldest and most prestigious shipbuilding company. It was going to be one hell of a merger, and photos of the glamorous couple frequently punctuated the society pages of the Sun.

No, Diz thought, as she gazed back at Clarissa's smoky gray eyes. There was no there, there for her.

Clarissa hung up her phone.

"What time are you leaving for the party?" she asked.

Diz shrugged. "Sometime after six. I figure it'll take forty-five minutes to get there with all the Christmas shoppers clogging the Metro."

This year's party was at Nevermore!—a high-end tapas bar at the Inner Harbor.

"You're taking the Metro? Why don't you take a cab?"

"A cab?" Diz raised an eyebrow. "Sure . . . I mean, I don't really have to eat the rest of the month."

Clarissa sighed. "Ride with me. I've got a car."

"Of course you do."

"Don't be a cretin. You'd be doing me a favor."

Diz was intrigued. "How so?"

Clarissa looked like she was trying to decide whether or not she wanted to answer that question.

"Oh, dear," Diz guessed. "Trouble in paradise? You and Dash Riprock have a falling out?"

"Go fuck yourself."

Diz sighed. "I usually do on Friday nights."

Clarissa shook her red head. "Why do I bother with you?"

Diz gave her a blinding smile. "Because I'm a foot taller than you, and whenever we go anyplace together, people think you're out with Rachel Maddow."

Clarissa thought about that. "Sad, but true."

"So." Diz adjusted the black horn-rims that used to make her look like a nerd, but now made her look chic. "What's up with Dash? He not coming to the party?"

Clarissa shrugged. "He has to work late."

"On the Friday night before Christmas? What? Is there a late-breaking shipment of yard arms coming in from Norway, or something?"

"Or something." Clarissa smiled. She had a great smile, with big, deep dimples that made Diz go weak at the knees if she looked at them for too long. It was every bit as hypnotic as staring at a lighted candle, and every bit as dangerous, too. If you weren't careful, you'd end up going blind.

Diz sat back in her chair and extended her long legs. She was wearing her best pair of red, high-top Chucks. They matched her suspenders perfectly. "Let me get this straight. You need me to keep you company until Lord Nelson arrives?"

"Something like that," Clarissa said.

"What makes you think I don't already have a date? Or two?"

Clarissa rolled her eyes. "If you do, I promise not to cramp your style. Besides, aren't you likelier to make friends with someone at the party? If memory serves, you fared quite well last year. What were their names, again?"

"I have no idea who you're talking about."

"Oh, yes, you do. I'm talking about those two zaftig types from the mail room."

Enlightenment dawned. "Oh. You mean Randi and Ronni. The twins. How could I forget?"

"Beats me," Clarissa offered. "You walked with a limp for nearly a week."

160

"And I thought you didn't care."

"In your dreams."

Clarissa had no idea how true that statement was.

"Well," Diz said. "It's true that I do like to keep my options open. So you're in luck. I don't, as it happens, have a date for tonight. Yet."

Clarissa smiled at her. "Great. Then maybe you'll consent to keep me company until Dane arrives?"

Diz narrowed her eyes. "I'm curious about something, Clar."

"What's that?"

"Why hang out with me? Why not just mosey on up to the head table, where the rest of the 'fambly' will be tossing back the single malts?"

"I don't socialize with my father at work."

"This isn't work. This is a Christmas party."

"Maybe for you. For me, it's work."

"Well that kind of sucks."

Clarissa shrugged. "I'm used to it."

Diz smiled at her sadly. "I know. That's the part that sucks."

Clarissa stared at her for a moment. She opened her mouth to say something when Marty Jacobs appeared in the doorway to their cube.

"Yo—Diz. A couple of us are gonna splurge and share a cab ride to the Harbor. Wanna come along?" He glanced at Clarissa, then lowered his voice. "Lisa even volunteered to sit on your lap if you promise not to behave."

Diz glanced at Clarissa, who seemed to be studying something fascinating on the sleeve of her jacket.

"No thanks, Marty. I've made other plans."

"Dude." Marty looked incredulous. "I don't think you heard me. I said Lisa, as in the woman voted Miss Sweater Meat of 2011."

"I heard you, Marty," Diz hissed. "Tell Lisa I'm beyond flattered, but I've made other plans."

Marty stood there looking back and forth between Diz and Clarissa. Then he shook his head. "Whatever floats your boat. Don't say I didn't ask."

"I won't."

"Later." He rapped the wall of their cube and backed out, headed for god knows where.

Diz looked at Clarissa who sat there regarding her with a raised eyebrow.

"Miss Sweater Meat?" she asked.

Diz shrugged.

Clarissa shook her head. "I guess it's an acquired taste."

Diz fought to keep her gaze away from the plunging neckline of Clarissa's silk blouse. Telling Clarissa that she could certainly hold her own in a Sweater Meat contest would probably be a bad idea.

A very bad idea.

"Yeah," she said instead. "I guess."

The party at Nevermore! was in full swing.

Or was that full swig?

Most of the management echelon decamped as soon as the dancing started.

Diz didn't really blame them. The majority of the dancers were beyond rhythmically challenged, and their obscene gyrations made them look like drunken extras from the set of Mogambo.

Across the table from her, Clarissa just looked amused. She was sipping on a glass of Pinot Noir, or Petit Syrah, or something red and expensive, and Diz was amazed at how long she could make one glass of anything last.

Diz was feeling no pain, and not just because of the five vodka gimlets she'd had. Dash/Dane was still a no-show, and Clarissa didn't really seem to mind, nor did she appear to be in any particular hurry to leave.

Diz could feel a surge of false courage pushing against the levy of better sense that normally kept her out of harm's way. And that couldn't be good news. After three drinks, Clarissa started to look less formidable. After five, she started looking downright . . . attainable. And Diz was barely clinging to enough good sense to realize that it was in everyone's best interest for her to change the circumstances—fast.

Idly, she wondered where Lisa was. Maybe it wasn't too late to rethink that whole lap-dance idea.

The music was so damn loud that it was hard to think. And she needed to be able to think. She needed to think because right now, all she wanted to do was act.

She heard Clarissa say something, but the ambient noise was too loud for her to make out what it was. She leaned toward her.

"What?" she bellowed.

Clarissa met her halfway. Bad idea. This was far too close for comfort. Her eyes were like tractor beams.

"I said, do you want to dance?" she repeated.

Diz looked around at the crush of people standing near their small table. No one seemed to be looking her way.

"With whom?" she asked.

Clarissa rolled her eyes. "With me, nimrod."

Diz wasn't sure she heard her correctly. "Did you say with you?"

"Is there an echo in here? Yes. Dance. You. With me."

Diz stared at Clarissa with her mouth hanging open.

"Oh, for god's sake," Clarissa finally said. She grabbed Diz by the hand and yanked her to her feet. "Come on. It won't kill you."

Diz could feel the room starting to spin.

"I'm not so sure this is a good idea," she said, as Clarissa pulled her toward the dance floor.

"I think you can handle it," she said, tightening her hold on Diz— probably so she couldn't fall. Or flee, which was likelier. "Be strong and courageous."

Diz wasn't feeling particularly strong right then, and she appeared to be leaking courage like a giant sieve.

Clarissa led them to a spot on the dance floor that was mostly unoccupied. Someone slammed into Diz from behind and shoved her up against Clarissa. She ended up with a mouthful of red hair, and Clarissa grabbed on to her suspenders with some kind of death grip. The sensation of having all that silk-clad sweater meat plastered up against her was making her woozy. She had a feeling that this wasn't going to end well.

The music changed. Lady Gaga now.

Great.

Red Wine. I've had a little bit too much.

Clarissa laughed. "This should be my theme song."

Diz could feel the vibration of her words against her ear. She drew back and looked at her. They weren't so much dancing as swaying. There wasn't really much room to move around.

"Seriously? You've had, like one glass, all night."

Clarissa rolled her eyes. "It's a metaphor, asshole."

Diz was confused. "For what?"

Clarissa just shook her head and tugged her closer. "You're a bright girl. Figure it out."

Diz was going to reply, but she got distracted when she noticed that people were staring at them. Lots of people. It started out small, then seemed to spread out across the dance floor like a wave. Between gyrations, they were pointing and talking behind their hands.

She bent closer to Clarissa's ear. "People are staring at us."

"You only just noticed that?" Clarissa replied.

Diz nodded. Clarissa's hair smelled great—like red violets.

"Why are they looking at us? Is my fly unzipped or something?"

Clarissa laughed. "Is your fly on your ass?"

Diz had to think about that. In fact, her fly was quite happily conjoined with the waistband of Clarissa's tight skirt. Right now, it was one hundred and eighty degrees away from her ass.

"No."

"Then I don't think it's related to your pants."

"Well what the hell is it then?"

Clarissa pulled back and gave Diz an ironic look. She raised a hand and ran it through Diz's thick head of short, dark hair.

"They think you're Rachel Maddow, nimrod."

"Oh." Diz had a sudden, and brief, moment of clarity. "That."

"Yeah. That."

"Lucky you."

Clarissa smiled and tugged her forward. "No argument from me on that one."

Someone slammed into them again. This time, the perpetrator stopped and apologized.

"Hey, sorry about that," he said.

Diz lowered her chin and looked at him over the rim of her glasses. He appeared to be anything but sorry.

"No problem," she said.

The guy continued to stand there, staring at them. "You're Rachel Maddow, aren't you? Man . . . I knew it was you. You totally don't look this tall on TV."

Clarissa started to laugh.

Diz rolled her eyes. "Well. You know how those cameras distort everything."

"This is so freaking cool," the guy said. "I don't really watch the news much, but I've seen you on Leno."

"Right," Diz said. "I'm really proudest of my late night TV work."

"Hey. I won't bug you anymore."

"Thanks," Diz said. She turned away from him and started to steer Clarissa off the dance floor.

"What's the matter, Rach?" Clarissa asked. "Don't you like dancing with me?"

"You call that dancing?" Diz asked. "It was more like roller derby. Why don't we just find a doorway to stand up in, or a deserted closet? At least we'd end up with fewer bruises."

"Well, that depends on what you have in mind," Clarissa said.

Diz stopped and stared at her. "Do I know you?"

"Not as well as you could." Clarissa gave her a look that could only be described as sultry. And Diz was sure about that because she checked. Twice.

Tunnel vision. Isn't that what it's called when everything around you suddenly constricts into a tiny pinhole through which you can see only one thing?

That's how Diz felt. And she wasn't sure if it was because of the booze, or due to the insane realization that she was moving in to kiss Clarissa—who halfway seemed to be inviting it.

"There you are," a voice behind them roared. "I've been looking all over this place for you."

Dash Riprock. Of course. He'd have to show up at precisely this moment.

Diz dropped her chin to her chest.

Clarissa didn't look exactly ecstatic to see him, either.

Dane Nelson looked like he'd just popped out of a ten-best list in G.Q. He looped an arm around Clarissa's shoulders and kissed her on the hair.

"Hi ya, babe. Sorry I'm late."

Diz noticed that he was holding a half-empty martini glass. Apparently he wasn't that desperate to find her.

Clarissa glanced at Diz, then looked back at Dane. "I gave up on you."

From your mouth to god's ear, honey.

Dane laughed, revealing a set of perfect teeth. They looked blue in the neon light.

"Hey, I got here as soon as I could." He looked around the crowded place. "Where's your stuff? I'm beat. Can we get out of here?"

"You remember Diz, don't you?" Clarissa asked.

Dane glanced at her. Diz could see his eyes moving up and down her frame.

"Sure. Hi, Diz. Thanks for keeping my girl company."

"No problem, Dash."

He didn't appear to notice the nickname, but Diz saw the corners of Clarissa's mouth twitch.

"Look," Diz said. "I'm kind of beat myself, Clar. I think I'll call it a night."

Clarissa looked disappointed. "You're leaving?"

Diz nodded. "You don't need a chaperone anymore, and I definitely don't need anything else to drink. I'll see you on Monday, okay?"

She started to turn away but Clarissa laid a hand on her arm.

"At least let us give you a ride home?" She looked at Dane, who took the hint.

"Oh. Sure. Yeah. We'd be happy to drop you off." He drained his glass and set it down on a nearby table.

Asshole.

"No thanks," Diz said. She looked around until she saw Marty holding up the bar. "I'll share a cab with Marty."

"And Lisa?" Clarissa asked.

Diz looked at her in surprise. Clarissa dropped her gaze.

"Maybe," she replied. "If I'm lucky." She held up a hand and gave them a brief salute.

She walked away, cursing herself for her stupidity. What the hell had she been thinking? Clarissa was just using her to kill time until Lord fucking Nelson showed up. And she had almost blown it. If Dane hadn't appeared precisely when he did, Diz would've ruined everything. Clarissa certainly would have slapped her, and tomorrow's headlines in the Huffington Post would've been all about how Rachel Maddow got dumped in a Baltimore nightclub.

Marty saw her and waved her over.

"Diz." He looked behind her. "Where's the Duchess?"

Diz jerked her head toward the door. "Prince Charming finally showed up."

"Sweet." He looked her over. "So you're finally on work release?" He signaled the bartender. "Let's have another round. What are you drinking? Gimlets?"

"Nothing else for me, dude. I'm already half toasted."

166

"Fuck that shit. It's Friday night, and the company is picking up the tab."

The bartender appeared.

"I'll have another T&T." Marty gestured at Diz. "And she'll have a Goose Gimlet." He looked at Diz and frowned at her morose expression. "Make hers a double."

"Jesus, Marty. You'll have to pour my ass into a cab."

"Yeah. So? What are friends for?" He raised his glass. "We'll have just one more drink, then we'll head out."

Right. Whatever.

Three drinks later, Diz was past the point of no return. She knew she was in trouble when a server reached over her to retrieve a platter of hot—something—from the bartender. The steam from the dish wafted up into her face, and she felt the room start to spin.

Marty saw it.

"Oh, Christ, you're gonna hurl, aren't you?" He quickly picked up his glass and pushed away from the bar.

Diz clapped a hand to her mouth and nodded. She slipped off her stool and staggered toward the restrooms, gaining speed as she pushed her way through the crowd, which parted like the Red Sea before the staff of Moses.

Apparently, she wasn't the first person to make this trip.

In the solitude of a bathroom stall, she let go of everything, including what was left of her hope and dignity. Then she sagged to the floor and cursed her miserable life.

This is what it always came down to, she thought. This is what you got if you let yourself believe in fairy tales.

A pair of heels appeared outside the stall. Someone tapped on her door.

Great.

"Just a second," Diz muttered. "I'll be right out."

She managed to haul herself to her feet and took a quick look to be sure there was no mess to clean up.

Diz always cleaned up her messes.

With shaking hands, she opened the door.

Clarissa was standing there.

Diz was stunned. Was this some kind of fresh delusion?

"You look like shit," Clarissa said, without a trace of empathy.

Nope.

She was real all right. And she was mad as hell. Her face looked like a thundercloud.

"What are you doing here?" Diz pushed past her and headed for the sink.

"I came back to get you. I had a feeling you'd do this."

"Do what?" Diz bent over the sink and rinsed out her mouth with cold water.

Clarissa walked up behind her. "This. Act like a stupid frat boy." She grabbed a stack of paper towels and reached around her to wet them. Then she wrung them out and pressed them to the back of Diz's neck. It felt great.

"Yeah, well . . . a propos of frat boys, where's Dash?"

Clarissa shrugged. "I dropped him off at home."

"Your home?"

"His home—not that it's any of your business."

Diz stood up and turned around to face her. Clarissa kept the damp towels against the back of her neck. That meant she continued to stand awfully close. As nice as that was, Diz felt like it was risky. Her stomach was still doing somersaults. The bright light in the bathroom was making her head swim. The scent of red violets wasn't helping much, either.

"I think I need to go lie down," she said.

Clarissa actually smiled. "You think?" She laid a hand on Diz's forearm. "Can you walk?"

Diz nodded.

"Let's go. My car is right out front."

Diz didn't have the stamina to argue with her. "Okay."

Five minutes later, Diz was snugly strapped into the soft leather passenger seat of Clarissa's Alfa Romeo.

They were driving along West Pratt Street, away from the harbor. Clarissa took a right on South Paca and drove past the main campus of the University of Baltimore.

"My home away from home," Diz muttered.

"What did you say," Clarissa asked.

Diz shook her head. "Nothing." She ran her hand along the wood grain dash of the car. "What is it with you and all the Italian stuff?"

Clarissa shrugged. "I like simplicity. I like beautiful things." She smiled. "I like things that are simply beautiful."

Diz snorted. "No kidding."

168

Clarissa looked at her. "No kidding."

Shit. There was that stomach thing again.

"I think you need to stop," she rasped.

Clarissa checked her rearview mirror, then roared over to the side of the road. "If you puke in this car, I'll kick your ass," she cautioned.

Diz was fumbling with her seatbelt.

"Jesus." Clarissa reached over and unhooked it. Red violets. It was too much. Diz fell out of the car and staggered to her feet. She made it as far as somebody's parked Mercedes, slid down the hood, and tossed her cookies all over its front tire.

She felt a set of cool hands on her forehead. They held on to her until she finished.

"Come on," Clarissa said. "We're almost there."

She helped Diz stand up and guided her back to the car.

"Where are you taking me?" Clarissa didn't live in this part of town. She lived in a high-rise condo, near Boston Street Pier.

"I'm taking you home."

"You know where I live?"

Clarissa looked at her. "Of course."

Diz wanted to ask how, but it was too complicated. She was amazed at her ability to be coherent at all.

"I don't suppose you have a bottle of Lavoris stashed somewhere in this thing, do you?" she asked.

Clarissa actually smiled. "No. But I think there might be some Tic Tacs in the glove box."

Diz opened it and fumbled around inside the uncommonly large compartment. Italians must have to carry a lot of shit around, she thought. She pulled out a rolled up pair of torn pantyhose.

She held them up. There was a gaping hole in the thigh area of the left leg.

"Care to explain these?" she asked.

Clarissa glanced at them. "No. I really don't."

"Hmmm. Okaaayyy."

"It's not what you think," Clarissa said.

"Since you don't know what I think, you don't really get to say that."

"I can imagine."

"I bet you can't."

Clarissa sighed. "Okay. What do you think?"

Diz rolled them back up. "I can only imagine two explanations. One—Dash was in an incredible hurry, and these got snagged on one of his diamond-studded cufflinks."

"You have a rich fantasy life, don't you?"

"I'm starting to develop one."

Clarissa shook her head. "What's your other explanation?"

"Ah. You wear these on your head while you indulge in your secret passion for knocking over mini-marts."

Clarissa thought about that for a moment. "I do love Twinkies."

Diz looked at her smugly. "Inspector Dupin's got nothin' on me."

She put the pantyhose back into the glove box and continued to rummage around until she found her prey.

"Voila." She pulled out a white plastic box and shook it. Then she held it up to read its label. "Oh, great. Citrus. Just what I need."

"Beggars can't be choosers, Diz."

Diz shook out a handful of the tiny mints and popped them into her mouth.

"Ugh. Maybe I should just chew the pantyhose?"

"I always knew you were a pervert."

Ten minutes later, they were parked in front of Diz's brick row house. Her condition had deteriorated dramatically. Clarissa got out and walked around to open her door.

"Keys?" she asked.

"Pocket," Diz said. She didn't carry a purse.

"You expect me to look for them?" Clarissa asked.

Diz nodded.

Clarissa sighed. "Stand up, then." She helped Diz climb out of the car.

Diz leaned against Clarissa as she fumbled around in her front pockets.

"This is kinda nice," Diz muttered against her hair.

"Don't get any ideas, nimrod."

"I won't," Diz promised. "Not any new ones, at least."

Clarissa held up the keys. She took hold of Diz's arm. "Can you make it up the steps?"

"I think so." Diz took a shaky step forward, then stopped.

"Oh, god, you're not going to be sick again, are you?" Clarissa asked with alarm.

"No. Just want to savor this. Can we go slow?"

Clarissa sighed. "Sure."

They slowly climbed the steps. Diz leaned heavily against Clarissa while she fumbled with the keys.

"If you don't have a car, why do you have so goddamn many keys?" she groused.

"You know, for someone with such a classy background, you sure do curse like a sailor."

"Yeah? Well it must be from spending two years in a basement with you."

Clarissa finally found the right key and unlocked the door. They stumbled inside. Clarissa stopped dead in her tracks while she looked around the spacious interior. It was tastefully appointed with primitive antiques and colorful artwork.

"Whatssamatter?" Diz asked.

"This place is gorgeous."

"You sound surprised."

Clarissa looked at her. In the soft lamplight, her eyes looked more hypnotic than usual, and that was saying a lot. Diz got an idea. Well, it was a repeat of the same idea she'd had earlier at the club. She leaned toward her, but gravity wasn't cooperating. She missed her target and kept going. Clarissa barely caught her.

"Come on, Casanova. Where's your bedroom?"

"That was fast," Diz slurred. "I was at least gonna make us drinks."

Damn, she smelled good. Diz dropped a sloppy kiss on her neck. "I really like you," she muttered.

Clarissa steered them toward the stairs. "I really like you, too. And I'll like you a whole lot more when I can get your clothes off. You smell like a brewery."

Diz continued to nuzzle her neck as they made halting progress up the stairs. "You wanna get me naked? I've always wanted to get you naked."

"Really? I hadn't noticed." Clarissa pushed Diz's hand away from her breast. "Step. Step. One more. That's right. You can do it."

You bet I can do it, Diz thought.

They were nearly at the top landing. Diz was feasting on her neck now. And she'd managed to work her free hand back inside Clarissa's jacket. It was soft and warm in there. Everything about Clarissa felt soft and warm.

Next thing she knew, she was falling backwards, and Clarissa was right on top of her. They landed on the bed with a soft thud. Clarissa pushed up on her forearms.

"Good god, you're a pain in the ass." She sat all the way up and straddled Diz. "And a heavy one, at that." She unhooked her suspenders and started to unbutton her white shirt. "Let's get these dirty clothes off you."

"I'm dirty?" Diz was busy groping any part of Clarissa she could reach.

Clarissa batted her hands away in between manipulating buttons and zippers. "Yes, you're dirty. And I must be crazy."

"Why are you crazy?" Diz asked with a yawn.

"Because," Clarissa pulled off Diz's shirt and backed away to tug down her trousers, "against all reason, I seem to like it."

Clarissa stood up next to the bed and removed Diz's shoes. Then she pulled her pants the rest of the way off. Diz was now clad only in her bra and panties. Clarissa hastily pulled a blanket up to cover her.

"You need to go to sleep now," she said. She removed Diz's glasses and put them on the nightstand.

"I don't wanna sleep." Diz reached for her. "I wanna snuggle."

"You want to snuggle?"

Diz nodded sleepily. "Please?"

Clarissa glanced at her watch.

"Please?" Diz made her biggest, puppy-dog eyes. "I promise to behave."

Clarissa rolled her eyes. "Sure you do."

"I promise, Clar." Diz yawned again.

Clarissa deliberated for a minute. Then she sighed and knelt on the edge of the bed. "Okay, but only for a minute. I mean it."

Diz smiled through her haze of inebriation and happy delusion. She held up the blanket in invitation.

"I must be in my dotage," Clarissa said as she kicked off her shoes and lay back against her.

Diz wrapped her up in her arms. God she felt great. They fit together perfectly.

"Clar?" she asked, stifling another yawn.

Clarissa turned her head on the pillow to look at her. Their noses were practically touching.

"What?" Her voice was soft and low.

"Thanks."

172

Then Clarissa kissed her. Or she kissed Clarissa. She wasn't sure which one of them started it, but it didn't really matter. The kiss went on and on, until Diz felt herself floating away. She was aware that her head had dropped onto Clarissa's shoulder, then she wasn't aware of anything but the faint, sweet scent of red violets.

When the morning came, Diz was sure of three things. One, she was alone in her bed. Two, something clearly had died in her mouth. And three, she would never drink eight vodka gimlets again. Ever.

She lay on her back and stared up at the ceiling of her bedroom. She had a vague recollection of Clarissa bringing her home, and an even vaguer recollection that she'd done some drunken groping on the stairs. She closed her eyes in mortification.

The longer she lay there, the more she remembered. One nightmare succeeded another until they were too numerous to count.

Oh, Jesus Christ. She undressed me.

Diz lifted the blanket and gazed down at her scantily clad form. Thank god. At least she still had her underwear on.

But there was something else. Clarissa had been on the bed with her. She was sure of it. And they kissed. She raised a shaky hand to her lips. She was sure of that, too.

Wasn't she?

Shit, who even knew? The whole thing could just be some kind of drunken wish fulfillment. It wouldn't be the first time for that. She was so damn pathetic.

She gingerly rolled over to test her equilibrium. Not too bad, considering.

She caught a trace of something on the pillow. Red violets. Holy shit. It was then that she saw the shoes . . . Jimmy Choo's . . . on the floor next to the nightstand. Clarissa's shoes.

Oh my god. She was here. She's still here.

Either that, or she left without her fucking shoes . . .

"You're awake."

Diz looked up at the doorway. Clarissa stood there, holding a tall glass of something. She walked to the bed.

"Can you sit up? How's your head?"

"Which one?" Diz pushed herself up into a sitting position and

173

tugged the blanket up to cover her chest.

"Here." Clarissa held out the glass. "Drink this."

Diz eyed her with suspicion. "What is it?"

"Don't ask. It's a home remedy. My father swears by it."

Diz recalled being amazed by the number of single malt Scotches Bernard Wiley blew through during the ninety minutes he tarried at the party last night. She supposed he probably knew some things about hangovers. She took the glass and sniffed at its contents, then recoiled in disgust.

"Jesus Christ. What is this? It smells like sweat and dirty feet."

"Just hold your nose and drink it. Then hop in the shower. I've got a nice, hot breakfast waiting for you downstairs."

Diz looked up at her. How was it possible for anyone to look so goddamn gorgeous in the morning? She'd shed her jacket, and was standing there in her skirt and un-tucked silk blouse.

"What are you still doing here?"

Clarissa shrugged. "I fell asleep. By the time I woke up, it didn't make sense to leave. Besides," she folded her arms, "I was worried about you."

"You were worried about me?"

Clarissa rolled her eyes. "Yes. I was afraid you might fall out of bed and drown in a pool of your own vomit."

Diz had to smile at that. "I can be pretty charming."

"I'm starting to figure that out," Clarissa said, drily.

Diz tried to wink at her, but the action made her head hurt. She raised a hand and rubbed the back of her neck.

"Just kill me now and get it over with," she said.

"You'll be fine." Clarissa nodded at the beverage. "Drink up."

Diz took a deep breath. "Bottoms up," she said, and drained the glass. Five seconds later, she wasn't sure if she wanted to die, or vomit, and then die.

"What the fuck was in that?" she rasped when she could find her voice. "Tar?"

Clarissa just smiled at her. "Shower now. Then come downstairs and eat something." She took the empty glass from Diz, turned around, picked up her shoes, and left the room.

Diz watched her go in amazement. Was any of this really happening? Clarissa actually seemed to be enjoying her little June Cleaver routine.

Of course, June Cleaver never looked quite that hot . . .

Whatever. Diz pushed the blanket aside and slowly got to her feet. So far so good. At least the room wasn't spinning. She made her way to the bathroom and looked at her reflection in the mirror.

Oh, god, she thought. Her eyes looked like a page from Google Maps, and her hair made Don King's look tame. Rachel Maddow could sue her for character defamation and win in a walk. Maybe Clarissa was right, and a shower would help.

She sure as shit hoped so.

In fact, the shower helped a lot. So did putting on some clean clothes. By the time Diz ventured back downstairs, she felt almost human again.

Clarissa had plugged in the lights on the Christmas tree. Diz always got a live tree, and this one was a beauty—a big Frasier Fir, trucked all the way in from the mountains of North Carolina. It was an eight-footer, and it proudly monopolized one corner of the big living room. The tree was decorated with blue and white lights, and hundreds of tiny paper ravens. It had taken her years to fold all the origami birds. It was something she started doing one late night in the stacks of the graduate library—a simple diversion to keep her awake while she drank from her thermos of coffee and tried to ignore the fact that she'd somehow have to show up for work in a few more hours. Year after year, her flock of ravens grew larger, and Diz bought bigger and bigger trees to accommodate them all. She vowed that when she finally finished her Ph.D., she'd stop folding ravens and add a cardinal to the mix—a bright and colorful period to end the longest, run-on sentence of her adult life.

Diz loved Christmas. Not a lot of people knew that about her.

There was music playing. Jazz. It sounded like Sophie Millman. Diz was impressed that Clarissa had figured out how to turn on her sound system. Usually she had to ferret out the goddamn instruction manual whenever she wanted to play it. Diz wasn't all that great with machines. She really belonged in another century. Well. All except for that whole wardrobe thing. Her friends all liked to tease her about how technically savvy she wasn't. She didn't even have an iPod. And shit . . . these days, most people had more iPods than they had chromosomes.

That was probably a good essay topic. Maybe she'd tackle that one after she finished writing her dissertation? Why not? Her company published Wired magazine. Maybe Clarissa could help her get an article placed?

Clarissa.

Diz still couldn't believe that she was here. She couldn't believe that any of last night had actually happened. She really wanted to ask Clarissa about how much of what she thought she recalled was real, but she felt ridiculous about doing so. Besides, if any of it had really happened, Clarissa probably just wanted to forget about it. Diz would only make it worse for both of them if she brought it up.

It was typical, she thought. She'd had the greatest night of her life with the woman who fueled most of her fantasies, and she was too drunk to be able to remember any it with certainty.

Of course, she thought, if she'd been sober, none of it would have happened in the first place.

It was a paradox. Like the rest of her life.

She crossed her living room and went into the kitchen. Clarissa was nowhere in evidence, but her small pub table was neatly set for two. And something smelled great. So. It appeared that Clarissa could cook, too. Diz smiled. The cranky redhead was now two-for-two in the June Cleaver Derby.

But where in the hell was she?

There were a finite number of places to look. She was either out back in the small courtyard that passed for a yard, or she was in Diz's study.

Nothing much doing in there, Diz thought. Unless, of course, you were into perusing your weight in extant primary source documents related to the rise of ratiocinative fiction. Somehow she doubted that Clarissa would find that very appealing. It even made her ass drag, and she was passionate about the stuff.

There was fresh coffee in the pot on the countertop. Diz poured herself a cup.

"I'm in here," Clarissa called out.

The voice was coming from her study—a small room adjacent to the kitchen.

Diz went in search of her.

Clarissa was sprawled out in her leather chair, reading something. She had a stack of loose-leaf pages piled up on the ottoman at her feet.

Diz recognized the open document box on the floor next to her chair.

Oh, god. It was her fucking dissertation.

She sighed and crossed the room. "I see you discovered nature's cure for insomnia?"

Clarissa held up the pages. "You mean this? I don't think so."

"No?" Diz perched on an old oak three-legged stool that sat near her chair.

Clarissa shook her head. "It's mesmerizing. I hope you don't mind?"

Diz shrugged. "If you were bored, you could've just watched The Home Shopping Network." Or gone home, she thought. Why was Clarissa still here?

"I wasn't bored. I was curious."

"Curious?" Diz asked. "About what?"

"Climate change," Clarissa said dryly. She added the pages she had been reading to the stack at her feet, then dropped them all into the box on the floor. She looked up at Diz with those smoky gray eyes that always spelled trouble. "What do you think I mean?"

Diz set her cup of coffee down on an end table. "To tell the truth, I don't know what to think about any of this."

"This?" Clarissa asked.

"Yeah." Diz was growing exasperated. "This." She wagged a finger back and forth between them. "Any of it. All of it."

Clarissa slid forward on her chair. "You're such a nimrod."

"I'm a nimrod?"

"Yes."

Diz felt like her head was starting to swim again, but it wasn't from her hangover. "Do me a favor, Clar. Don't make me work to figure anything out today. I'm only firing on about half of my cylinders right now."

Clarissa grabbed her by the shirtfront. "Come over here and sit down." She pulled her over to the ottoman.

Diz was afraid to look at her. She had a sneaking suspicion that if she did, she'd give too much away. Either that, or she'd turn into a pillar of salt.

It was pretty much even money.

"I'm sorry about what happened last night," she said.

Clarissa was quiet for a minute. "Which part?"

Diz looked up at her. "Take your pick."

In the background, Sophie Millman wrapped up her set, and the next CD in the changer started to play. Strains from "Orinoco Flow" filled up the quiet space between them.

Clarissa turned her head toward the sound. "Is that Enya?"

Diz nodded.

"You're certainly full of surprises," she said.

"Is that good or bad?"

"Does it have to be one or the other?"

Diz shrugged.

"What's the matter?" Clarissa asked.

"I feel ridiculous."

"Why?"

"Why?" Diz repeated. "Because I acted like an idiot."

Clarissa looked like she was trying hard not to smile. "You always act like an idiot."

Diz narrowed her eyes. "You were here last night, right? I mean, I didn't imagine that part, did I?"

"Oh, no," Clarissa agreed. "I was here, all right."

"And did I or did I not . . . well . . . you know?"

Clarissa looked confused. "Did you or did you not what?"

"Jesus, Clar." Diz's mortification was increasing with every second that passed. "Did I or did I not kiss you?"

Clarissa gazed up at the ceiling as she pondered her answer. "No. I remember a fair amount of clumsy, drunken groping on your part, and a few vague murmurings about finding my sweater meat, but I don't remember that happening."

Diz felt her heart sink. She looked away to hide the blush she knew was on its way.

So it had all been a drunken fantasy. And she had just added insult to injury by being stupid enough to confess it. How in the hell would she ever recover from this one?

She felt a warm hand on her thigh. She looked back at Clarissa, who was regarding her with a strange little smile on her face.

"You know, you're actually kind of cute when you're riddled with self doubt."

"Gee. Thanks."

Clarissa sighed. "For someone who's such an expert on detective fiction, you sure manage to miss a lot of big clues."

"What's that supposed to mean?"

"Seriously? You can't figure it out? I thought you were some kind of Rhodes Scholar?"

Diz rolled her eyes. "That wasn't me, that was Rachel Maddow."

Clarissa just looked amused.

Diz was now on the other side of exasperated. "You really enjoy fucking with me, don't you?"

Clarissa was studying her with those hypnotic eyes. "I'll admit it's an idea that's been gaining some traction lately."

Diz looked at her in surprise.

A timer went off in the kitchen.

"Come on." Clarissa got to her feet. "Let's get you something to eat."

She left the study and headed into the kitchen.

Diz allowed herself to sit there another minute, marinating in her misery, before she stood up, adjusted her hair shirt, and followed the faint but hopeless trail of red violets that led to the world's most unattainable woman.

Clarissa left right after breakfast.

She said she had some "things to take care of," and that she was meeting Lord Nelson at two o'clock.

But Clarissa had been right, and the food really did make Diz feel better. The bacon and Gruyere quiche with leeks and sun-dried tomatoes was sumptuous. Diz ate two large pieces.

"I didn't know you could cook," she said after her first bite.

Clarissa shrugged. "I do all right."

"All right? This is fabulous."

"Don't give me too much credit. You had all the ingredients."

That was true. Diz liked to cook, too.

Clarissa looked around her kitchen. "This really is a beautiful place."

"I was lucky to find it," Diz said. "The former owners get most of the credit for the improvements."

Clarissa looked at her. "Did they sell it to you furnished, too?"

"Well . . . no."

"I've actually been thinking about moving to a new place."

Diz was surprised. Clarissa lived in one of the most desirable, waterfront areas of Baltimore. Condos in her building went for over a million dollars, easy.

"Why?" she asked.

"I don't know," Clarissa said. "Maybe because I spend my days below street level and my nights in the clouds." She shrugged. "I think I'd prefer to live my life someplace in the middle."

Diz smiled at her. "It does have its advantages."

"In your case? I can only imagine."

Diz narrowed her eyes. "What's that supposed to mean?"

"Well," Clarissa explained, "I'm sure it's a real benefit to only have to stumble down a couple of steps when you feel compelled to vomit on someone's expensive, German sedan. I'd have to take a ten minute elevator ride to enjoy that privilege."

Diz sighed. "Remind me to include that feature in the ad if I ever decide to put this place on the market."

Clarissa smiled and finished her coffee. Then she glanced at her watch.

"I really do have to go." She gestured at their dishes. "Help me clear this away?"

Diz waved a hand over it. "No. I've got this. Go ahead and take off."

"You sure?"

Diz nodded.

Clarissa stood up, and Diz followed suit. "I'll see you out."

They walked to the front door. Diz helped Clarissa into her jacket.

"I really don't know how to thank you," she said. "Believe it or not, this doesn't really happen very often."

"Really?" Clarissa grabbed hold of her mane of red hair and pulled it free from the collar of her jacket—a cascade of red violets filled up the tiny foyer were they stood. "You don't often have overnight guests?"

Diz was embarrassed. "Well . . . no. But that isn't really what I meant."

"Relax, Casanova. I know what you meant."

"Well." Diz stood there stupidly, staring at her shoes and not really knowing what to say. She felt ridiculous and exposed—like she was trying to get up the nerve to ask the prom queen if she could carry her books to homeroom.

Clarissa sighed.

Diz raised her eyes and looked at her.

Clarissa's expression was unreadable. "I'm sure I'll regret this."

Diz was confused. "Regret what?"

"You wanted to know if you kissed me last night?"

Diz nodded.

"And I told you I didn't remember that happening?"

Diz felt her misery compounding. Why was Clarissa bringing this up again? It was like grinding salt into an open wound.

"But," Clarissa took a step closer—the cloud of red violets moving with her, "what I didn't tell you is that I do remember this happening."

Clarissa pushed Diz up against the wall and laid one on her. And it wasn't any kind of tentative, you're-drunk-and-won't-remember-this, experimental kind of kiss, either. It was a full-out, head-on, hands-down, hang-ten, hail Mary, all-over-but-the-shoutin' kind of kiss that left nothing to the imagination. And if Clarissa hadn't had such a good handhold on her forearms, Diz would've slid to the floor and ended up in a pool of red violets on the rug.

"Holy shit," Diz said when she finally came up for air.

"Now I'm really going to be late," Clarissa said. She seemed out of breath, too. "See you tomorrow?"

Tomorrow was Christmas Eve. Diz nodded stupidly.

Clarissa kissed her again—quickly this time—then turned toward the door. She was halfway out, then stopped and faced Diz. "What the hell is your real name, anyway?"

Diz smiled sheepishly. "Maryann."

Clarissa raised an eyebrow. "Maryann?"

Diz nodded.

"Christ. Clarissa and Maryann. We sound like a lost episode of Little House on the Prairie."

Diz gave her a cocky grin. "Strange bedfellows?"

"You've certainly got that part right." She walked down the steps toward her waiting car. "I'll call you later."

Diz stood in the doorway and watched her leave. Then she went outside and sat down on the top step. It was cold today. The sliver of sky that was visible above the canopy of trees that lined her street looked bleak. The street was wet. Diz held out a hand. Tiny snowflakes landed on her palm. It looked like it was going to be a white Christmas.

She smiled through her haze of confusion and elation. Nothing about what was happening made any kind of sense.

A cardinal landed on the wrought iron railing that flanked the steps to her row house. Diz and the bright red bird stared at each other through the gauzy curtain of swirling snow.

Last night had been surreal. Today was on the other side of surreal. And tomorrow? Tomorrow was Christmas Eve. Christmas Eve with Clarissa. She sure never saw that one coming.

Clarissa was right. Sometimes Diz did miss the biggest clues.

But it didn't really matter, because, right now, all the omens were looking good.

She gazed at the bright red bird that continued to perch there staring back at her. Here he was, impossibly ahead of schedule. A talisman to signify the end of her darkest days . . . like the icon at the end of a string of rosary beads.

"Hope is the thing with feathers." Isn't that what Emily Dickinson said?

She smiled at the crimson metaphor, and extended her hand.

"Hello, gorgeous."

About the Author

ANN McMAN is the author of six novels, *Jericho, Dust, Aftermath, Hoosier Daddy, Festival Nurse* and *Backcast,* and the short story collections *Sidecar* and *Three.* She is a recipient of the Alice B. Lavender Certificate for Outstanding Debut Novel, and a two-time winner of the Golden Crown Literary Award for short story collections. Her novel, *Hoosier Daddy,* was a 2014 Lambda Literary Award finalist. She resides in Winston-Salem, North Carolina with her wife, two dogs, two cats, and an exhaustive supply of vacuum cleaner bags.

Backcast

"*Backcast* is a memorable story about the unbreakable strength and resilience of women. Skillfully executed, the story is easy to become emotionally invested in, with characters that are guaranteed to entertain and enthrall."   —*Lambda Literary Review*

"I love Ann McMan."
              —Dorothy Allison, author of *Bastard Out of Carolina*

Backcast by Ann McMan
Print 978-1-61294-063-2
Ebook 978-1-61294-064-9

www.bywaterbooks.com

the one that got away

"Every page of Carol Rosenfeld's novel delivers delectable dykedrama, replete with the quagmires of sexual obsession, high-stakes betrayal, and lesbian holiness. How can I laugh so hard at these characters and simultaneously feel tenderness for each and every one? Rosenfeld's fierce wit is addictive; I read the book in one go."

–LUCY JANE BLEDSOE, author of *The Big Bang Symphony*

The One That Got Away
Print 978-1-61294-060-1
Ebook 978-1-61294-618-8

www.bywaterbooks.com

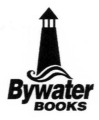

Bywater
BOOKS

At Bywater Books we love good books about lesbians just like you do, and we're committed to bringing the best of contemporary lesbian writing to our avid readers. Our editorial team is dedicated to finding and developing outstanding writers who create books you won't want to put down.

We sponsor the Bywater Prize for Fiction to help with this quest. Each prize winner receives $1,000 and publication of their novel. We have already discovered amazing writers like Jill Malone, Sally Bellerose, and Hilary Sloin through the Bywater Prize. Which exciting new writer will we find next?

For more information about Bywater Books and the annual Bywater Prize for Fiction, please visit our website.

www.bywaterbooks.com